TAKING CHANCES

TIMBER RIDGE RIDERS
∽ Book Seven ∾

TAKING CHANCES

Maggie Dana

PAGEWORKS PRESS

ISBN 978-0-9851504-6-4

Edited by Judith Cardanha
Cover by Margaret Sunter
Interior design by Anne Honeywood
Published by Pageworks Press
Text set in Sabon

For Barbara

1

THREE DAYS BEFORE CHRISTMAS a stranger walked into the barn as if she owned the place. She wore city clothes—dark gray suit, crisp white blouse, and high-heeled boots that had no business being within fifty yards of a horse. Under one arm, she carried a red brief case. It made an odd splash of color.

"Who's *that*?" Kate McGregor asked her best friend, Holly Chapman.

Holly grinned. "Santa's attorney?"

Trying not to be obvious, Kate peeked through the bars of Tapestry's stall. The woman's lips were blue with cold, and no wonder—it was below freezing outside, with two feet of snow on the ground and icicles the size of pitchforks hanging from the gutters. The city woman had no coat, no gloves, or even a designer scarf. She looked ready for a board meeting in New York, not a barn in the mountains of Vermont.

Holly's mother, Liz Chapman, emerged from the tack room. Her faded jeans had patches on both knees and there was a smudge of saddle soap across her freckled cheeks. "Welcome to Timber Ridge," she said, wiping her hands on a cloth. "You must be—"

City Woman sniffed. "Where's the horse?"

Flinching at the woman's bad manners, Kate patted her mare's copper-colored neck and leaned over the heavy wood partition that separated her from Magician, Holly's black gelding. "Which horse is she talking about?" Kate asked Holly.

There were two dozen horses in the barn, all the way from fat little Plug who taught the beginner kids to ride, to the enormous, slow-moving Marmalade who made everyone except Brad Piretti—the high school's star quarterback—look short. In between were the riding team's horses and several that belonged to boarders.

"You got me," Holly said, shoving a hunk of blond hair off her face. It fell forward again and she tied it back with a braiding elastic.

Kate scooped up another forkful of manure, dumped it into her muck bucket, and watched Liz guide the stranger toward Skywalker's stall. The big bay snorted and tossed his head. He belonged to Angela Dean but she hadn't ridden him since the last horse show. He'd been cooped up for a week and was probably itching to bust loose.

City Woman kept her distance. "Viola said this horse will be absolutely perfect for my niece."

"Who's Viola?" Kate whispered.

"Angela's mother," Holly whispered back.

Kate had never heard Mrs. Dean's first name before. To everyone at the barn she was Mrs. Dean, just like the women in a Jane Austen novel, except they were a whole lot nicer than Mrs. Dean. Kate glanced at the newcomer, then at Angela's restless horse. As usual, Skywalker was pacing his stall like an impatient toddler. Angela refused to let him out in the paddock because he'd roll and get muddy and then she'd have to groom him.

Clipping a lead rope to Skywalker's halter, Liz led him into the aisle. City Woman moved even further from the horse and narrowly missed tripping over a broom.

Kate stifled a laugh. Holly sniggered.

They had a perfect view, half-hidden in their horses' stalls and pretending to muck them out when their attention was firmly riveted on the newcomer. Nobody this gossip-worthy had come to the barn since Angela's short-lived trainer, who'd departed under a cloud of suspicion at the end of August.

"How old is your niece?" Liz said, keeping a firm

grip on Skywalker. Angela's horse was doing his best imitation of a Mexican jumping bean.

"Thirteen," the woman said. "She rides at Northbrook Farm."

Holly let out a muffled squeak. "Wow!"

"Double wow," Kate muttered.

For years, Northbrook had produced more top-level riders than any other barn in New England. Everyone wanted to ride there, but Northbrook took only the best of the best and only if they could afford it. Kate slipped out of Tapestry's stall. She looked at Skywalker, now beginning to work up a sweat. The whites of his eyes showed.

Liz said, "Kate, get his tack for me, would you?"

"Sure," Kate said.

"I'll help," Holly added.

Kate headed for the tack room with Holly right behind her. They scooted inside and shut the door. Kate leaned against it, bursting with questions.

"What's going on?" she said. "Is Angela selling Skywalker?"

"Looks like it," Holly said. "She's due for an upgrade."

For a moment, Kate just stared at her. Never in a million years would she ever sell Tapestry, no matter how much money anyone offered. It would be like cutting off her arm or selling her best friend. Unthinkable, totally unthinkable.

"But why?" she said. "I thought Skywalker was Angela's ticket to the big time—you know, Young Riders, the United States Equestrian Team?"

"The Olympics?" Holly said, grinning.

Kate nodded, because that's what Mrs. Dean always said. She'd blabbed about it so many times on Facebook and Twitter that people who didn't know any better actually believed her. Photos of Angela in a classical dressage outfit appeared all over the web, even though she'd never ridden beyond first level. The trouble was, Mrs. Dean didn't know one end of a horse from the other. All she knew was whatever Angela told her.

Holly pulled Skywalker's saddle off its rack. "If Angela's getting herself a new horse, it's because of you."

"*Me?*" Kate said. "What have *I* done?"

"You've been beating her all season," Holly said. "Mrs. Dean expects Angela to win everything, and she's not doing it with Skywalker."

"But *you* beat her at the last show," Kate said. "Not me."

"On *your* horse," Holly reminded her.

As Kate reached for Angela's bridle, her mind backtracked to the previous weekend. Magician had balked at loading on the horse trailer so they'd taken Tapestry along to keep him happy. But shortly before Magician's first class, a runaway horse plowed into him and Magician pulled up lame, so Holly had ridden Tapestry instead because Kate wasn't allowed to. She'd been barred from riding in the show, thanks to Mrs. Dean who'd invoked an obscure rule in the Timber Ridge bylaws that said anyone who competed for the team had to be a resident.

And Kate no longer was.

She'd moved out of the Chapmans' house shortly before Thanksgiving after living there all summer while her dad was researching rare butterflies in Brazil. He'd rented a nearby cottage just for the winter, so they'd have to move again in the spring.

Kate desperately wanted to buy a house at Timber Ridge, but they were all wickedly expensive . . . like *astronomically* expensive. No way could her father afford one, especially after he'd sunk all his money into "Dancing Wings," a local butterfly museum that he hoped to expand into a research center for entomology students and people who loved bugs. Kate was fine with bugs, but spiders freaked her out. If her father ever came home with a tarantula, she'd—

"C'mon," Holly said. "Let's go and find out for sure."

* * *

Liz had removed Skywalker's blanket by the time they returned with his tack. Gently, Kate hefted his saddle into place, made sure the fleece pad wasn't wrinkled, and wiped mud off his girth before doing it up. Angela's tack was always grubby unless she'd managed to con someone else into cleaning it for her.

"How big is he?" the city woman said.

"Sixteen-two," Liz replied.

City Woman sighed. "In English, please."

"He's sixty-six inches at the withers," Liz said.

"The *what?*"

While Liz explained patiently how horses were measured, Kate adjusted Angela's stirrup leathers to fit Liz's much longer legs and helped Holly put Skywalker's bridle on. He mouthed the double bit, spitting flecks of foam onto his neck and shoulders.

City Woman eyed them suspiciously. "Is he sick?"

"No," Liz said. "He's fine."

"Mom, is Angela selling Skywalker?" Holly blurted.

Her mother hesitated. "Yes."

"So why isn't she here?" Holly said. "It's her job to show off her own horse."

"Angela's in Colorado," Liz replied. "Skiing."

Kate shared a look with Holly. So that's why Angela

had missed the last two days of school. Her cousin Courtney hadn't been there either and neither had Kristina James, the team's newest rider. Maybe they'd all gone together. But why Colorado, when they lived a short walk from some of the finest skiing in New England?

Liz took Skywalker's reins and was about put her foot in the stirrup when City Woman said she wanted one of the girls to ride him instead.

"You," she said, pointing at Kate. "You're the same height as my niece."

There was a long pause, then Liz said, "Kate, are you okay with this?"

"Yeah," Kate said. "I guess so."

She'd never ridden Skywalker before, but for Liz's sake, she'd give it her best shot. If she didn't put on a good show with Angela's horse, Mrs. Dean would blame Liz. She had come close to losing her job more than once because of Mrs. Dean's constant meddling in how the barn was run.

Holly handed Kate a helmet. "Good luck."

"Thanks," she said as Holly gave her an elastic as well. Kate scooped her thick brown hair into a low pony tail and crammed the helmet on top. "I'll probably need it."

"The helmet or the luck?" Holly said.

"Both," Kate said, mounting Skywalker. He was a

push-button horse, but you had to know which buttons to push. Half the time, Angela got them wrong. At the last show, Skywalker blew holes in his dressage routine by acting like a total spaz, but he surprised everyone with a brilliant performance over the show jumping course.

"Take it slowly," Liz warned, as Kate followed her into the arena. "He takes a while to settle down."

She set up a few jumps while Kate rode Skywalker in serpentines and big circles. Fighting the bit, he tossed his head and skittered sideways like a crab.

"Inside leg," Liz called out. "Keep him focused and on the rail." She stood in the middle of the arena, both hands in her pockets. It wasn't much warmer inside than it was outside, and Kate was grateful for the down vest she wore over her body protector and the for leather riding gloves that Holly had made her put on. She'd given them to Holly for her fifteenth birthday the previous month.

Keeping a light touch on the reins, Kate sat deep in the saddle and drove Skywalker forward with her legs. Angela rarely did this. She acted more like a passenger than a rider and always kept him under tight control, as if she were scared he'd run away with her. Finally, after twenty minutes of patient schooling, Skywalker dropped his nose and accepted the bit.

"Nice," Liz said. "He's listening to you."

He was also looking good. Skywalker's sleek summer coat shone like polished mahogany because Angela kept him blanketed and inside. He hadn't grown a shaggy winter coat like the other horses that spent most of their time outdoors. Kate trotted past the observation room where Holly sat with City Woman, who looked as if she'd rather be anywhere else but in a barn.

Holly gave Kate a discreet thumbs-up.

Maybe she'd be able to get more information, like details about the niece and how much they were offering for Skywalker. Kate's experience with buying a horse was limited to the auction where she got Tapestry for a few hundred dollars. Skywalker had to be worth ten thousand. Probably more. With a talented rider, he could easily become a star.

After Liz gave the nod, Kate popped Angela's horse over the brush jump, followed by the crossrail. Skywalker jumped without hesitation and seemed eager for more. So Kate aimed him at the double oxer, and he cleared it with inches to spare. They flew over the parallel bars and the red brick wall as if they were no bigger than shoe boxes. Slowing to a trot, Kate patted Skywalker's sweaty neck.

Angela was crazy to sell this horse.

He was a winner.

City Woman obviously thought so, too, even though she had no clue what she was looking at. By the time Kate cooled Skywalker off and rode him back into the barn, City Woman's checkbook was already out. Kate felt her mouth drop open. How could anyone who knew nothing about horses decide to shell out thousands of dollars to buy one? City Woman obviously had more money than sense.

"What did she say?" Kate said, as Liz ushered City Woman into her office. The door closed behind them with a quiet click.

"Not much," Holly said.

"Didn't you ask questions?"

"Of course I did," Holly replied.

Kate led Skywalker into his stall and took off his tack. "So?"

Holly shrugged. "Her niece is some sort of genius on horseback, and her parents can't afford to buy her the right horse. So City Woman is doing it for them."

"Without a vet check?" Kate said.

"Mom said Dr. Fleming was at the barn yesterday," Holly said. "Maybe he checked Skywalker then." She threw a blanket over Angela's horse and fastened the buckles. "I guess City Woman's in a big rush. She must want to have him gift-wrapped in time for her niece to open on Christmas morning."

"Lucky girl," Kate said.

She'd known girls like this at her old barn in Connecticut. Kate had mucked their horses' stalls and cleaned their tack to earn enough money for her own riding lessons. When the rich girls were on vacation in places like Hawaii and the Caribbean, Kate had exercised their expensive horses and tried not to feel jealous.

"You guys looked great out there," Holly said.

"Thanks." Kate checked Skywalker's water and fluffed up his bedding. He seemed kind of lonely, so Kate gave him a hug. At first he stiffened, then let out a cautious sigh as if he didn't know quite what to do with a little bit of affection.

Holly frowned. "Hey, do you suppose Mrs. Dean planned things this way?"

"Planned what?" Kate said, still hugging Angela's horse. He'd begun to relax and was nuzzling her pocket for a treat. She pulled out half a carrot and fed it to him.

"Making sure that Angela wasn't around when a serious buyer showed up," Holly said.

"That's crazy talk," Kate said.

"I'm serious," Holly replied. "Think about it. Some days Angela rides like a dream, and—"

"—sometimes she flops about like a sack of potatoes," Kate finished.

Holly nodded. "So, if Mrs. Dean wants to sell Sky-walker, she knows Angela might flub it up, right?"

"I guess," Kate said.

"Which means," Holly went on, "Mrs. Dean didn't want Angela anywhere near the barn when City Woman arrived. She wanted my mom or one of us to handle it."

All of Kate's instincts rebelled. Angela treated her like dirt, so what was she doing helping Angela to sell her horse? Kate caught her breath and tried to put herself in Angela's shoes.

Mrs. Dean demanded perfection.

She got seriously angry if Angela lost a tennis tournament or blew a ski race, and she went totally ballistic if Angela didn't win blue ribbons at every horse show. Kate couldn't imagine having a mother like that. Her mom had supported her until the day she died.

A tear escaped down Kate's cheek.

For a few soggy minutes, she felt sorry for Angela. She was a victim of her mother's ambition. But was it her ambition, too? Nobody knew what Angela really wanted because she kept herself buttoned up and pretended not to care. She didn't seem to care much about the horses she rode, either, because the next afternoon Northbrook's blue-and-white trailer arrived to collect Skywalker and Angela wasn't even there to say goodbye.

2

RUMORS ABOUT SKYWALKER'S DEPARTURE spread through the barn faster than gossip at the high school. One of the younger kids announced that Santa was giving Skywalker to a little girl who loved horses more than Angela did. Another insisted he'd gone to live with Marcia Dean, Angela's ten-year-old stepsister who'd moved to New York with her father.

"Nuh-uh," said Marcia's best friend, Laura Gardner, who'd already been down to visit her. "They don't have room in their apartment for a horse."

The riding team speculated wildly.

"I bet Angela's quit," said Sue Piretti as she brushed Tara, her Appaloosa mare. "She's totally freaked out that Kate's beating her, so—"

"Wrong," said Jennifer West from inside Rebel's stall. The chestnut gelding nudged her as if he agreed. "She's been grounded."

"Why?" said Robin Shapiro.

Jennifer sighed. "For losing."

"That makes no sense," Robin replied, putting her gray mare, Chantilly, on the crossties. "If Mrs. Dean grounded Angela, she wouldn't be skiing in Colorado with Courtney and Kristina."

"Okay," Sue said. "But—"

The girls argued back and forth as if it were a high school debate and the winner would get an award. Kate glanced at Holly, who was grooming Tapestry. Nobody, not even Liz, knew what was going on. They wouldn't find out until after the New Year when Angela got back from Colorado. Not having her around was the best Christmas present ever.

Well, not really. But it was a huge relief.

Ever since Kate arrived at Timber Ridge, Angela and her mother had tried to force her out, and they'd almost succeeded. But now, here she was, grooming Holly's horse and preparing to ride him in the next qualifying show. This was thanks to Mrs. Dean who'd pulled a bunch of strings and gotten the rules changed to benefit her daughter. Riders no longer had to be part of a team;

they could compete as individuals which gave Angela a second chance at qualifying for the prestigious Festival of Horses show in April.

It also gave Kate another chance. But she couldn't ride her own horse because Tapestry had already qualified with Holly and wasn't allowed to compete again with a different rider.

"No problem," Holly had declared gleefully in front of Angela. "Kate can ride Magician instead."

Grabbing a hoof pick, Kate leaned into Magician. There was no sign of his earlier lameness. She ran a hand down his hind leg and he obliged by lifting his foot. As Kate bent to pick it out, she heard the stall door slide open.

"Hey," said Brad Piretti. "May I come in?"

"Sure," Kate said, straightening.

Snow dusted the broad shoulders of Brad's ski jacket. Lift tickets hung from zippers and brightly colored patches covered the front like bumper stickers on a minivan. One of them said, *Born to Shred.*

Brad pulled off his enormous mittens and patted Magician's rump. "Holly says you're riding him in the next competition." He smiled at her. "That's really cool."

"Yes," Kate said, suddenly tongue-tied.

She'd been friends with Sue's elder brother since Halloween. He'd just begun taking riding lessons and had come to help out at the last show. Kate had tried to hide her disappointment at not being allowed to compete, but Brad had seen right through it. He'd taken her skiing the next day to help take her mind off it.

He'd also asked her out a couple of times, but so far Kate had managed to side step the issue. She didn't want to hurt Brad's feelings, but she already had a boyfriend—well, sort of. His name was Nathan Crane and Kate hadn't seen him in almost four months because he was an actor shooting a film in New Zealand. They'd met when part of the *Moonlight* movie was shot at Timber Ridge and Kate had ridden as a stunt double for Nathan's glamorous co-star, Tess O'Donnell.

The girls at school envied Kate for having a movie-star boyfriend, but they had no clue how complicated it really was. Ordinary dates were impossible. Even a carefully orchestrated trip to Alfie's Pizza had turned into a mob-fest. Nathan had worn a false beard and sunglasses, but his fans weren't fooled. They swarmed like bees and begged for his autograph, thrusting menus and paper napkins—even their arms—at him to sign.

Nathan had laughed it off. He was used to it. But Kate wasn't. She hated being the center of attention unless it came with a horse and even then, she usually blushed and didn't know what to say, which was happening right now because Brad was telling her what a great rider she was and how she'd beat Angela in the next show. Kate felt herself turning red.

"You'll win," Brad said. "No problem."

Kate was about to tell him that all bets were off because Angela was getting a new horse, but then she stopped herself. They didn't know for sure this would happen, and if it did, would it be in time for the next show? Besides, it wasn't about winning; it was about qualifying for the finals in April.

Brad cleared his throat. "Do you want to come skiing again? We could go next week," he said. "Or I could teach you to snowboard instead."

"Yes," she said.

He grinned. "Is that 'yes' for skiing or 'yes' for snowboarding?"

"Skiing," Kate said, grinning back. Her first lesson with Brad had been loads of fun, even if her legs had complained afterward. She wanted to get good enough to ski with Jennifer and Sue on the black diamond runs they were always raving about. One of them was called *Devil's Leap.*

"It's gnarly," Jennifer had warned.

Sue added, "With moguls the size of Volkswagens."

Kate had no idea what a *mogul* was. Was it some sort of business tycoon, like Angela Dean's stepfather? He was a financial wizard on Wall Street, and he'd helped

Kate's dad finance the butterfly museum. Liz had called him a mogul.

"What's a mogul?" she said.

Brad waved his arms in the shape of a dome. "Huge lumps in the snow," he said, "made by skiers carving turns."

"Like big furrows?"

"Yeah, pretty much," he said. "Only way bigger, more like—"

"Volkswagens?" Kate said.

Brad burst out laughing. "Good one," he said. "So, how about—?"

Kate's cell phone rang. It was probably her father, wondering when to pick her up. She fished it out of her pocket, but it wasn't Dad—it was Nathan. His timing was awful; somehow he always managed to call when Brad Piretti was around. It was almost as if he had a sixth sense about it.

"Sorry," Kate mumbled and turned away.

"What are you sorry about?" There was a hint of doubt in Nathan's voice.

"Nothing," Kate said, blushing even harder. She hadn't talked to Nathan in over a month. He sounded different, kind of like he'd gotten a New Zealand accent or something. "Where are you?"

"Home," he said.

For a minute Kate thought Nathan meant Vermont. It was where he'd grown up, going to school with Holly's boyfriend, Adam Randolph, and he always called it "home" when they talked and texted.

Then it registered.

Of course. Nathan was back in California where his family now lived, but only for a few days. As soon as Christmas was over, he would be heading for New Zealand again to finish filming. They hoped to wrap it all up by the middle of February, and he'd be sending her tickets for the New York premiere in April.

"You *are* coming, aren't you?" he said.

"Yes," Kate said, as Brad clumped out of Magician's stall.

* * *

"You're not being fair," Holly said, as she led Tapestry into the indoor arena.

Kate followed with Magician. They'd agreed to swap horses for as long as Kate was getting ready for the next show. Then she and Magician would be thoroughly comfortable with each other by the end of January.

The other girls were already warming up their horses. Sue and Jennifer rode in opposite circles at the far end of the arena while Robin trotted Chantilly along the rail. Brad Piretti, Kate was relieved to see, gave her a thumbs-up from the observation room which meant he couldn't have been upset by Nathan's phone call. And why would he?

It wasn't as if she were dating Brad.

Kate tightened Magician's girth and stuck her foot in the stirrup. "What about?"

"Brad and Nathan," Holly said.

Kate turned to glance at her. "Huh?"

"You can't date both of them at once."

"I'm not," Kate said, climbing onto Holly's horse. "Brad's just a friend."

"Does he know that?" Holly said.

"Yeah, I think so," Kate said. This whole boy thing confused her. Why couldn't you just have a guy for a friend, the way she and Holly were friends?

"But you don't *know* so," Holly said, mounting Tapestry. She gathered up her reins and pinned Kate with a look. Holly's bright blue eyes never missed a trick.

For a moment, Kate shriveled.

Holly's infamous looks were more withering than her mother's, and those were bad enough. Liz pricked holes in overblown egos faster than you could pop a balloon. But she was always fair about it. She never made anyone feel small or stupid, even Angela, who deserved it more than most.

Jennifer trotted by on Rebel, followed by Sue and

Robin. From the center of the ring, Liz called for attention.

"Listen up," she said.

Kate looked at Holly, but the moment was lost. They'd have to talk about this later. Or maybe not. Kate wasn't sure she was actually ready to talk about it—not even to her best friend.

She could talk to Holly for hours about horses and Holly's boyfriend, Adam, who also loved horses. But when it came to Kate and the guys she liked, Kate clammed up. Somehow, it didn't feel right, dragging her feelings into the open about stuff she didn't quite understand herself.

* * *

Nathan called on Christmas Eve. Kate was kind of expecting his call but it still felt like a special surprise. She was in the barn, getting ready for the riding team's party. Earlier, she'd helped Holly hang wreaths on the windows and held the ladder while Sue tacked pine boughs around the arena's double doors. Jennifer had decorated the tack room with tiny white lights. They twinkled among saddle racks and bridle pegs, turning the mundane into magic.

A huge carrot cake—made by Robin's mother—sat on a folding table outside Liz's office. The little kids stood around it, holding plates and forks and waiting for the okay to dive in.

"Merry Christmas," Nathan said, before finishing their conversation and hanging up. "I miss you."

"Me, too," Kate replied.

She'd never had a boyfriend before and had agonized over sending him a gift. Nathan was a movie star. He had almost everything, so what could Kate possibly give him that he didn't already have? In the end, she'd sent him a geeky t-shirt because Holly said she really needed to.

"He'll send you a gift," Holly said. "Trust me."

Sure enough, it had arrived via FedEx that morning—a black sweatshirt with a picture of Kate on the front wearing a floaty white dress and riding Magician straight toward the camera. Beneath it were the words, *Moonlight Princess*.

Is that how Nathan thought of her?

Kate stared at her muck boots, her grubby jeans. She wasn't much of a princess, but Holly was. She loved anything that glittered—eye shadow, nail polish, and t-shirts in a rainbow of colors. Her favorite books had sparkly vampires and unicorns on the covers.

"This is way cool," Holly said. She held up Kate's sweatshirt and danced around the tack room with it. "Wear it tonight for the party."

So Kate did, feeling ridiculously embarrassed, and

Holly took a picture of her and emailed it to Nathan right away. At that moment, Holly's boyfriend showed up with Brad Piretti. Kate, who'd been about to change back into her barn clothes, felt herself blushing redder than the pom-pom on Brad's ski hat.

"Nice shirt," he said.

From the barn's loudspeakers came "Rudolph the Red Nosed Reindeer." Jennifer led Rebel down the aisle. The chestnut gelding sported horns and Jennifer wore a shiny red nose that flashed on and off like a firefly. Wearing Santa hats, Sue and Robin skipped from side to side, dropping apples and carrots into each horse's feed bucket. Adam tucked a sprig of holly into Holly's ponytail, then kissed her cheek. To Kate's surprise, Holly turned faintly pink.

It began to snow again.

Liz hitched Marmalade to the sleigh. Harness bells jingled as she took the wide-eyed little kids for a ride. They circled the barn twice and came back to give the older kids a turn. Holly, Kate, and Adam climbed into the rear seat, followed by Brad who sat down beside Kate. He laid a blanket over their laps and she forgot all about Nathan and being embarrassed. She didn't even squirm when Brad casually draped his arm around her shoulders.

They were about to take off when her father drove

up. Kate asked Liz to wait. She wanted Dad to join them, but she changed her mind when a woman clambered awkwardly out of his car—first one elbow, then the other, and finally emerging like an overgrown stork from its egg.

"What's *she* doing here?" Kate said.

"Duh-uh," Holly said. "Mrs. Gordon volunteers at your dad's museum on Thursdays, remember?"

Kate had lost all track of time. It didn't feel like a Thursday. It felt like Christmas Eve, and it was going to be the best Christmas ever because she'd be spending it with Holly and Liz, along with her father. For once, he'd be home and not chasing butterflies in a remote jungle somewhere south of the equator.

"Oh, right," she said, groaning.

Mrs. Gordon had been really helpful to Dad, but she was also the high school principal. Kids called her "The Gorgon" because she had clouds of frizzy black hair, buggy eyes, and teeth like tombstones. She wore vintage clothes and shawls with lots of fringe that looked as if moths had been snacking on them, which they probably had. Mrs. Gordon was an amateur lepidopterist. She loved moths and butterflies as much as Kate's father did, and she'd encouraged him to buy the museum. He must've felt obliged to invite her to the barn's Christmas party. That's all it was.

Or was it?

Kate shared an anxious look with Holly. They'd been conspiring to get their parents together since Halloween, just like in Holly's favorite movie, *The Parent Trap*. Kate's dad hadn't dated anyone since her mom died five years ago. And Liz hadn't dated anyone recently either. She'd been a widow for almost three years and Holly insisted that she'd never even looked at another man until Ben McGregor moved into the village.

"Don't worry," Holly said, as Kate's father led Mrs. Gordon toward them. "She's not his type. Besides, she's married."

"Not any more," Kate muttered.

Holly stared at her. "What do you mean?"

"Dad told me she's getting a divorce."

3

HOLLY'S HEART SANK LIKE A BAG OF HAMMERS. She clenched her fists and shot a worried look at Adam.

He frowned. "What's wrong?"

"I'll tell you later," Holly said.

Up front, her mother was shifting over to make room for Ben and Mrs. Gordon. There were now seven people on the sleigh—a heavy load for one horse. Holly grabbed Adam's hand.

"C'mon," she said. "We'll take the next ride."

The sleigh lurched forward. Marmalade was as strong as an ox. He could probably pull ten people without breaking a sweat, but only if he felt like it. If you wanted him to trot on a Thursday, you had to start asking him on Monday because he needed time to think about it.

Most days, he barely moved.

Still holding Adam's hand, Holly leaped off the sleigh and headed for the barn. The music had switched to "Jingle Bell Rock," and Adam twirled her all the way down the aisle until she was positively dizzy. She almost forgot what she wanted to tell him, especially when he held up a piece of mistletoe and kissed her cheek again.

"So what's up?" he said, running a hand through his mop of blond hair. His green eyes twinkled with fun and reminded her of Nathan. They'd been best friends in school and looked so much alike that they'd often swapped clothes just to confuse their teachers.

Pulling herself together, Holly tried to explain how she and Kate wanted their parents to fall in love and get married so that Kate could live at Timber Ridge and be part of the riding team.

"But The Gorgon's ruining *everything*," Holly said, and flopped onto a bale of hay that promptly split in half. Someone had obviously cut the twine.

Laughing, Adam sat down beside her. "You can't manipulate people like that."

"Why not?" Holly grumbled. "It worked in the movie."

"That's not real life, you dodo."

Holly scowled at him. Adam knew all about *The Parent Trap* because she'd made him watch it three times already. He'd threatened to barf popcorn all over her if she forced him to sit through it again.

"It's all make-believe," Adam said, as if to drive the point home.

He was right, of course, but Holly refused to admit it. Stubbornly, she clung to this dream, the way she'd once clung to her dream of walking again after being hurt in the accident that had killed her father. People said it was impossible. But Holly had proved them all wrong. After being stuck in a wheelchair for two years she'd learned to walk—and to ride Magician again.

People had said that was impossible, too.

She was about to remind Adam that if you believe in something long enough and hard enough, you might just be able to make it come true, when Brad and Kate walked into the barn. Trailing behind were Kate's dad and the high school principal. They stopped to admire Cody, Kristina James's flashy palomino. He stuck his nose over the stall door and dripped slobber onto Mrs. Gordon's moth-eaten shawl.

Holly wanted to hug him. "Why did you bring The Gorgon in here?" she whispered to Kate.

"Dad wants to show her the horses."

"She's seen them before," Holly said.

Mrs. Gordon had shown up at the hunter pace where Angela cheated her way into first place, dragging Kate

with her. Kate had blown the whistle on her riding partner, causing the judges to reverse their decision, and
Angela had been trying to get even with Kate ever since.

She'd turned on Holly as well by wrecking her surprise birthday party. Somehow, Angela and Courtney
managed to mess up the sound system, but it spiraled out
of control. The fire alarms all blared at once and the
sprinklers doused everything, including the magnificent
cake that Jennifer's mother had made.

Cake?

Laura Gardner wandered by, mouth covered in frost-
ing. At the snack table, the other little kids were quietly
scarfing up the rest of Mrs. Shapiro's delicious carrot
cake. At least it looked delicious. Holly hadn't gotten so
much as a crumb.

She rarely got cake. Her mother was a genius with
horses, but she was hopeless when it came to measuring
cups and spatulas. Kate's father was even worse, so the
girls had pooled their money and bought both parents
cooking lessons for Christmas. It was part of the overall
plan to bring them together. With luck, Liz and Ben
would bond over learning to chop onions without chop-
ping off their fingers.

Right now, Holly wanted to chop off Mrs. Gordon's
bony fingers. They were resting like claws on Professor
McGregor's arm as if she owned him.

* * *

Kate woke up on Christmas morning filled with excitement. Except for Nathan, she'd have all her favorite people together for the day, including Bea Parker, Liz's old riding instructor. She used to breed horses, then switched to writing mysteries and knitting the most amazing socks. Kate hoped she'd get a pair for Christmas.

Persy, the black kitten, was draped warmly across her shoulders purring like a toy motor boat. He came with the cottage. It belonged to Aunt Marion, and she'd loaned it to Kate and her father for the winter. From downstairs came the sound of Dad making coffee. With luck, he wouldn't attempt scrambled eggs and bacon. The last time he did, Kate had spent an hour scraping burned bits off the frying pan.

Easing Persy gently to one side, Kate climbed out of bed. The kitten gave an elaborate yawn and went back to sleep, snuggled up in the pony-print comforter that Holly was letting Kate use until she got one of her own. A comforter just like it was on Kate's Christmas list, along with suede chaps and a winter blanket for Tapestry. She'd been borrowing one of Magician's old blankets and it was about to fall apart.

After a quick shower, Kate pulled on her jeans and Nathan's sweatshirt, then picked up the bag of gifts she'd be taking to Holly's house—a dressage manual for Liz, sheepskin slippers for Dad, multicolored sock yarn for Aunt Bea, and a silver curb-chain bracelet for Holly.

But that wasn't Holly's only gift.

With Nathan's help, Kate had managed to buy a special edition of the first *Moonlight* book, complete with the famous author's autograph.

To Holly, it said. *Best wishes, Yolanda Quinn.*

Nathan had even promised to introduce them to Yolanda Quinn at the movie's premiere in April. Kate couldn't wait to tell Holly about it. She would totally flip out.

* * *

When Kate and her father arrived at the Chapmans' house, Bea Parker let out a delighted whoop and pulled Kate into a bone-crunching hug. Kate caught a whiff of fresh herbs which meant Aunt Bea had taken charge of the kitchen, the way she had at Thanksgiving.

Holly said, "Come and see our tree."

It sparkled with tinsel, silver horse shoes, and a gazillion fairy lights. Popcorn and dried cranberries looped among tiny gold frames filled with photos of all the barn's horses. Miniature sleighs and painted wooden ponies dangled from the tips of branches. On top of the tree stood a magnificent black unicorn with outspread wings and a glittering horn. In its mouth was a bright orange carrot.

"Magician?" Kate said.

Holly grinned. "Who else?"

* * *

They'd almost finished opening presents when there was a knock at the front door.

"Is that Adam?" Kate said, running her hands over the gorgeous tan chaps that Liz had given her. She'd tried them on and they fit like they were custom-made, as did Aunt Bea's amazing socks. Dad had given her a winter blanket for Tapestry. He'd obviously consulted with Holly because it was the absolutely perfect shade of blue for a chestnut horse. She and Holly hadn't yet opened each other's gifts because they'd agreed to do it last and both at the same time. Kate couldn't wait to see the look on Holly's face when she saw the autographed book.

"He's not coming till tomorrow," Holly said.

"Is he bringing Domino?" Kate said. Adam rode for Larchwood Stables, where the next show would be held at the end of January. He'd already qualified for the finals on his half-Arabian pinto.

"You bet," Holly said.

There was another knock, louder this time. Liz

jumped off the couch, scattering tissue paper and ribbons like confetti. "This must be Cecilly."

"Who?" Kate and Holly said together.

But Liz was already at the door. She yanked it open and Mrs. Gordon swept into the house swathed in a long scarlet cape.

"It's the wolf," Holly growled, "disguised as Little Red Riding Hood."

Kate cracked up. She couldn't help it. But it wasn't that funny. With The Gorgon here, their carefully laid plans about getting Dad and Liz together had just taken another tumble.

* * *

"Why, Mom?" Holly said. "Why did you invite her? This is a family holiday not a high-school field trip." She'd managed to corner her mother in the kitchen while she was getting a cup of coffee for Mrs. Gordon.

"Just a splash of cream please, with a half teaspoon of sugar," The Gorgon had said, flashing a toothy grin at Kate's dad. From the look on his face, he was as surprised as they were over Mrs. Gordon's unexpected arrival.

Liz pulled her best china from the top cupboard. "I invited Cecilly because she has nowhere else to go," she said. "It's Christmas. People shouldn't be alone at Christmas. It's not right."

"It's not right that we're stuck with her, either," Holly muttered, but Mom didn't hear. She was too busy arranging a dainty cup and saucer on a tray, along with a real cloth napkin. Holly wanted to throw up.

"Get me a silver teaspoon from the cutlery box," Liz said. "There's one in there, somewhere."

"No, there isn't," Holly said, handing her mother an everyday spoon. "It's in the barn. You used it to measure Plug's worming medicine, remember?"

She hadn't really.

Worming medicine came in a tube and you squirted it directly into the horse's mouth. Holly shot an exasperated look at Kate while her mother poured coffee and carefully added the right amount of cream and sugar, per instructions.

The Gorgon had that effect on people. She was a teacher, the high-school principal. Even adults who hadn't had her for ninth grade biology wound up back-pedaling into obedient childhood whenever Mrs. Gordon was around.

Aunt Bea strode into the kitchen and plucked her striped apron from a hook on the wall. "Need any help?"

"No," Liz said, gathering up her tray.

"Yes," chorused the girls.

"In that case," said Aunt Bea, "Liz can go and entertain her guest while I chop vegetables with Holly and Kate."

"But we haven't finished opening—"

"Later," Aunt Bea said. "We'll take a break from the gifts, okay? You've already been spoiled rotten." She closed the kitchen door behind Liz and leaned against it. "Okay, what's got you two in a swivet?" There was a pause. "Although I can probably guess."

They took turns explaining Mrs. Gordon to Aunt Bea. "She's chasing after Kate's dad," Holly finished.

"Any fool could see that," replied Aunt Bea. "So what are you going to do about it?"

"That's it," Holly wailed. "We don't know."

"I do," said Aunt Bea.

"What?"

"You do absolutely nothing."

Holly opened her mouth, but the words got stuck in her throat. Aunt Bea was worse than Adam. He'd told her pretty much the same thing.

"Why?" Kate said.

"Because you can't interfere," Aunt Bea replied.

"What about the cooking course?" Holly said.

It had been Aunt Bea's suggestion. She'd even offered to help pay for it, but Kate and Holly managed on their own. Last night, Holly had put the final touches to a gift certificate she'd designed for Mom and Kate's dad and then had hidden it inside her sock drawer. She hadn't left it beneath the Christmas tree because it would get lost amid the mess of boxes and wrapping paper.

"Give it to them later," said Aunt Bea, "when your mother's guest has gone home." She rummaged in the drawer for a potato peeler and gave it to Holly, then pointed to a colander full of carrots and told Kate to wash them. "I doubt Cecilly will be here all night."

"Will you?" Kate said.

"Yes," she said. "I'm here for another two days, and if I catch either of you acting snarky or rolling your eyes behind Mrs. Gordon's back, I won't tell you about *The Barn Bratz.*"

"Are we in it?" Holly said.

Aunt Bea was writing a mystery series for kids, and she'd promised to include characters based on Holly and Kate. There'd also be lots of fabulous horses and a mean girl, just like Angela. Holly couldn't wait to read it.

"If you behave yourselves," Aunt Bea said, "you'll find out. If not, then—" With a mischievous grin, she held up her apron like a dance partner and waltzed around the kitchen table.

Holly bit back a smile. Aunt Bea's curly red hair, her wild imagination, and her flowery dress reminded her of Ms. Frizzle in *The Magic School Bus.*

4

WHEN MRS. GORDON FINALLY LEFT, Kate heaved a sigh of relief. It hadn't been easy following Aunt Bea's orders about being polite to the high school principal. Mrs. Gordon wasn't a bad person; she was just a bit weird.

After two glasses of wine, she'd gotten even weirder by inviting the girls to call her Cecilly. Kate was fine with calling Holly's mom Liz, and even Holly was getting used to calling Dad by his first name . . . but Mrs. Gordon?

Cecilly?

As soon as the door closed behind her, Holly shot beneath the tree and pulled out a large box that she dumped in front of Kate. The tag said, *To my best friend, EVER,* and was underlined three times. With a big grin,

Kate handed Holly a sparkly gift bag containing the special edition of *Moonlight* and Holly's curb-chain bracelet.

"One, two, three ... go," they said.

Ribbons and bows flew in all directions as both girls tore into their gifts. Kate pulled a pony-print comforter from its nest of tissue and immediately wrapped herself up in it, while Holly squealed with delight over her bracelet and the autographed book.

"I can't believe this," Holly said, peering at Yolanda Quinn's elegant signature. "Is it real? I mean, you didn't fake it, did you?"

"Duh-uh," Kate said. "I can't write that neatly."

"True," Holly said, as she dug out one last gift and tossed it toward Kate.

"What's this?"

"For Tapestry," Holly replied. "But you can open it for her."

Slowly, Kate untied the ribbons. Inside the box was a V-shaped browband with a row of tiny pearls, just like the one that went missing at the Fox Meadow Show.

"Wow! Thank you," Kate said. "It's perfect."

"Well," Liz said, "it looks as if we're done." Dropping to her knees, she began to tidy up the mess, and Kate suddenly remembered the special gift from her and

Holly. Was it buried in all the paper and boxes scattered beneath the tree? If so, they'd never find it.

"Where is it?" She nudged Holly.

"What?"

"You *know*." Kate pretended to stir something.

Holly slapped her forehead, then jumped up and ran down the hall toward her bedroom. Moments later, she returned with a large white envelope almost obliterated by an enormous silver bow and a dozen curly ribbons.

"Mom," Holly said, pointing to the couch where Kate's father was sipping a glass of red wine. "Sit next to Ben."

He moved over to make room. Liz settled herself beside him, a puzzled look on her face. Holly thrust the envelope toward them. "It's a gift . . . from both of us."

"Merry Christmas," Kate added.

Liz glanced at Ben. "What's going on?"

"I haven't got a clue," he said.

Holly gave a dramatic sigh. "Just open it, okay?"

One by one, Liz pulled off the ribbons and Kate held her breath. Maybe this wasn't such a great idea. Maybe her dad and Holly's mom would be upset that the girls had assumed they'd actually want to take cooking lessons together.

"I did the ribbons," Liz said, handing their gift to Ben. "Now you can open the envelope."

Slowly, Ben ran his finger beneath the flap. He flipped it open and waited, looking at Holly and Kate, but not pulling out the certificate.

"It's like the Oscars," Holly said.

"Only worse," Kate muttered.

Aunt Bea grinned. "And the winner is ..."

With a flourish worthy of Hollywood, Kate's father pulled out the elaborate gift certificate that Holly had made. It had blue ribbons and gold seals and a photo of Liz and Ben wearing chef's hats.

"Wow, Liz said. "How'd you do that?"

"Photoshop."

"And I helped," Kate said.

They'd spent hours going through the photos they took at Thanksgiving to find just the right one that wouldn't look too cheesy when Holly added the white toques. For extra measure, she'd Photoshopped a wooden spoon into Liz's hand and a carving knife into Ben's and set both parents behind a butcher-block table piled with cookbooks, a mixing bowl, and two cutting boards.

"His and hers," said Aunt Bea. "It's absolutely perfect."

There was an awkward silence and Kate felt for sure that they'd gone too far. Then her father burst out laughing, and so did Liz.

"They've really got our number, haven't they, Ben," she said, wiping her eyes.

He nodded so vigorously that his glasses fell off and landed in his beard. "And then some."

"So," Liz said, "shall we do it?"

"We'd better," Ben said, shoving his glasses back on. "It's a conspiracy."

"Yeah," Liz said. "It's the kids' way of telling us they don't want to starve."

She pulled Holly and Kate into a group hug. Then Kate's father joined in. Awkwardly, he wrapped his arms around all of them and reminded Kate of the days when her mom was alive and Dad would yell, "Pig pile," and they'd all collapse on top of each other in a flurry of arms and legs.

Aunt Bea took pictures.

Kate felt Holly's hand squeeze hers. She squeezed back. For a few precious moments, they were the family Kate and her best friend wanted.

* * *

Kate's inner glow lasted until she and her dad were halfway back to their cottage. He coughed a couple of times and said, "Don't tell anyone, but Mrs. Gordon's retiring."

"From what?" Kate said. Mrs. Gordon didn't look

old enough to be retiring from anything. She didn't even have wrinkles or gray hair.

"Your school," Ben said. "There'll be an announcement when you go back. The vice principal is taking over until the school board hires a replacement."

For a moment, Kate was stunned. She'd only been at Winfield High School since September, but Mrs. Gordon—even if she was a bit off the wall—was a permanent fixture that Kate had taken for granted, kind of like the cafeteria's awful pizza and gym lockers that refused to lock properly.

"So, what's she gonna do?" Kate said, with a sneaking suspicion she wasn't going to like the answer.

"She'll be working at the museum a bit more."

"Like how much?" Kate said.

She helped her father at the museum three afternoons a week and on Sunday mornings. It was part of their agreement: She swept the floors and tidied the museum's gift shop in return for Dad paying Tapestry's room and board at the barn.

"Pretty much full time," her father said, yanking the wheel to avoid a snow drift. "Cecilly will handle the financial end of things and help me set up the academic programs." He shot a quick glance at Kate. "Hey, maybe she'd like to join Liz and me on the cooking course. That would be fun."

"No, it wouldn't," Kate blurted.

She clapped a hand over her mouth. Had she really said that out loud? From her father's puzzled expression she obviously had, and they drove the rest of the way home in tight-lipped silence.

* * *

Adam and Holly were in the tack room when Kate arrived at the barn the next day. She could hear them giggling as she dawdled along the aisle.

To buy more time, she hung about feeding carrots to Tapestry and Magician. Then Adam's horse, Domino, stuck his head over the stall door and whickered, so Kate fed him the last carrot and stroked his handsome nose. She wasn't looking forward to telling Holly about Mrs. Gordon's new job. Dad had said not to tell, but she absolutely *had* to tell somebody.

"Chill out," Adam said, once Kate had stumbled through her explanation. "Your father's not going to fall for that old bat."

"Don't be too sure," Holly warned. "She'll be under his nose all day, and Kate's father is witless about women."

"How do you know?"

"Because Kate told me," Holly said.

Kate cringed. It wasn't just her father. She was witless, too—well, about boys—so maybe it was a family trait. If Brad Piretti asked her out again, she'd probably get all tongue-tied like she had the first time.

Half of her wanted to go on a date with him; the other half wanted to run away and hide. Holly wasn't much help either. Yesterday, when Kate finally worked up enough nerve to ask for advice, Holly had said, "Do whatever feels right."

Big help *that* was.

Kate had no problem with Brad teaching her to ski and having hot chocolate with him in the lodge afterward. It was when he invited her to the movies or out for a pizza, like on their own, that she turned shy and awkward.

As if conjured up by her thoughts, Brad Piretti appeared. His cheeks were flushed, and his curly brown hair was frosted with snow. He'd probably just gotten through snowboarding or helping his father groom the ski trails. He ducked his head to avoid hitting the doorframe and was barely inside the tack room when Adam told him about Mrs. Gordon.

Holly glared at her boyfriend. "It's a secret, you idiot."

"Not any more," Brad said, holding up his cell phone. "I heard about it ten minutes ago."

"Who from?" Kate said.

"One of the cheerleaders," Brad said. "They're texting about it like crazy. I reckon the whole village knows by now." He gave a little shrug. "I bet even Angela and Courtney know, too."

So much for Dad's big secret.

Kate grabbed her grooming box. She wanted to get a couple of hours on Magician before Liz took over the indoor arena with lessons for the younger kids.

Brad offered to help. "I'm getting pretty good with a curry comb," he said, hefting Magician's saddle and bridle into his arms. "And I'm a wiz at brushing forelocks."

"That's because you're tall enough to reach them," Holly said. "The rest of us midgets have to stand on a box."

"Hey, speak for yourself," Adam said.

He was almost six feet tall and still growing, but he only came up to Brad's eyebrows. Brad was still growing, too. He was already being scouted by college basketball teams but he said he had no interest. It was football and snowboarding for him.

And now riding.

Holly insisted it was because of Kate. That's why Brad was taking lessons on Marmalade and hanging out at the barn. Kate was flattered at first but then flustered, because she didn't know how to handle it. Plus there was Nathan. True, he wasn't around most of the time; but when he was, Kate loved being with him.

But it was getting harder and harder to have a relationship with someone who was always half a world away, to say nothing of trying not to believe the silly rumors that hit the gossip mags every week about Nathan and Tess.

Holly told her to ignore them.

"You busy tomorrow?" Brad asked, running a rubber curry comb over Magician's hindquarters. Magician shifted sideways from the force behind Brad's powerful strokes. It was probably like being groomed by a snow blower.

"Easy," Kate reminded him. "Horses are big, but they're sensitive."

"Like me?"

Despite Brad's grin, Kate knew he was serious. Sue had already warned her about his thin skin, which is why Kate felt so bad about turning him down.

"So, how about another skiing lesson tomorrow morning?" Brad went on, still currying Magician but not nearly as hard. Holly's horse gave what sounded like a sigh of relief.

Kate hesitated. She'd promised to help her father but

that was before he'd dropped the bombshell about Mrs. Gordon. Maybe she'd just play hooky and leave the high school principal to sweep the museum's lobby and tidy up its gift shop on her own.

"Okay, yes," Kate said. "I'd love it. What time?"

* * *

Brad's parents ran the Timber Ridge ski resort and refused to let Kate pay for her lift ticket and rentals. Sue confided that they never charged the riding team—except for Angela. She could afford to pay full price. "So don't tell her you're skiing for free," she warned.

Kate shoved her feet into yet another pair of ski boots. She'd already tried on a half dozen without finding a good fit. "Don't worry," she said, wincing. "Angela and I aren't exactly best friends."

"Duh-uh," Sue said. Her reddish-brown curls flopped forward as she bent to fasten Kate's buckles. "How do these feel?"

"Better, I think." Standing up, Kate rammed her heels down hard on the floor, the way Brad had shown her. Ski boots felt a whole lot different than riding boots but they had one thing in common: They were both impossible to walk in.

From a rack on the wall, Sue selected a pair of skis— green with white stripes, the Timber Ridge colors—and a set of matching poles. Kate hefted them over her shoulder and followed Sue outside.

Clothed in candy-colored outfits, a group of nursery school kids snow-plowed down the bunny hill. Hotdog skiers carved expert turns around them and made spectacular hockey stops that sprayed snow over anyone within ten feet. Overhead, the gondola's cable cars rumbled like distant thunder as they carried skiers and snowboarders to the peak of Timber Ridge Mountain.

"There's Brad," Sue said.

Wearing aviator shades, her brother stood beside the gondola base. Kate had ridden Tapestry beneath its lift towers many times with Holly, but this was totally different. She'd be hundreds of feet above the ground in a gaudy metal pod the shape of a bicycle helmet.

She gulped. "I can't go up there."

"You're good enough," Sue replied. "Brad said you're a natural."

"At falling over," Kate said. "The first time I managed to get off the bunny chair without crashing, the lift operator applauded."

"Don't worry," Sue said. "There are green circles all the way down."

"Promise?" Kate said.

From studying the map, she'd learned that green circles showed the easy trails, blue squares meant intermediate slopes, and black diamonds marked the toughest, like *Devil's Leap* and another horror named *Jaws of Death* that even Brad admitted was a challenge.

"You all set to go?" he said.

Kate swallowed her fear. If Brad could get on a horse and trot around the arena, the least she could do was climb into a gondola. "Yeah, okay."

Each brightly colored car held four skiers. When it was time to load, the lift attendant took their skis and shoved them into the racks of a shiny orange pod. Clutching her poles, Kate clambered into it behind Brad and Sue. The door slid shut. Purple polka dots covered the interior walls; orange stripes—just like the ones on Brad's jacket—zigzagged across the domed ceiling. Kate felt as if she were inside a giant Easter egg.

And then they were off—Sue sitting beside her, with her brother opposite. Kate could see herself reflected in Brad's sunglasses. He grinned at her, and she relaxed. Nothing would go wrong as long as she stuck with him.

5

As they approached the peak, Kate caught her breath. Spread out like a miniature forest, just the tips of tall pine trees showed above the deep snow. "Those don't look real," she said.

"They're not," Brad said. "We put them up every year to fool the tourists."

"And Santa," Sue added.

Brad grinned. "He'll be out any minute. Keep an eye on those trees over there. I bet he's waiting for just the right moment, and—"

"But Christmas is over," Kate said.

"Not up here," Sue said. "It's Christmas every day. Right up till Valentine's Day, St. Patrick's Day, and Easter."

"That's when we bring out the hearts, the shamrocks, and the eggs," Brad said.

Sue rolled her eyes. "You forgot New Year's Day."

"Father Time?" Brad said.

"He's too old to ski."

While they joked back and forth, Kate looked down. On the wide trail beneath them she saw a flash of color—hot pink, lime green, and the electric purple of Jennifer's latest hairdo. She and Robin were skiing with some friends from school. They'd gone up on the gondola about ten minutes before and were already heading for the black diamond runs. Jennifer stopped in midturn, looked up, and waved her ski poles. They matched her hair.

Kate waved back.

Later they'd meet at the half-pipe where Brad would swap his skis for a snowboard. Kate was looking forward to watching him perform flips, spins, and somersaults. Holly said he was totally awesome. She didn't ski, but Adam did. He was spending the week with Brad's family, and when he wasn't riding with Holly he was taking snowboarding lessons from Brad.

Stepping off the slow-moving gondola was a whole lot easier than skiing off a chairlift. Kate retrieved her skis from the rack, and within moments she found herself in a fairytale landscape filled with glittering icicles, frosted fir trees, and fluffy white snow that sparkled in the bright sunlight.

"Let's go," Sue yelled.

After making sure Kate was all set, Brad followed. Behind him, Kate felt her confidence rising. Sue was right. This green trail was easy and gentle and not the least bit crowded. Kate had plenty of room to turn without bashing into anyone else. Her skis left curvy imprints in the well-groomed snow.

All too soon the trail ended, and Kate followed her friends onto a narrower one. She leaned into her turns the way Brad had taught her and didn't even falter when they skied over a couple of low bumps.

"Whoopee," Sue cried, catching air.

Trees, stumps, and rocks whizzed by. Kate didn't think she'd ever gone this fast before—not on her own two feet, anyway. Perhaps on a horse, like when she was galloping Tapestry across the meadow or jumping Magician over the hunt course. But then she was always worried they'd stumble into a rabbit hole and break a leg, or—

Her skis hit a patch of loose powder. The tips crossed and Kate flew head over heels into a snow bank. Gasping for breath, she struggled to sit upright. Her skis had come off and were beginning to slide down the hill on their own.

Brad scooped them up. "Are you all right?"

"I think so," Kate said.

Cautiously, she wiggled both legs and arms. Nothing seemed to be broken—except for her pride. She'd been doing so well, too. Holding out his hand, Brad hauled Kate to her feet. Then he stood on her skis and anchored them perpendicular to the slope so she could step into her bindings without fear of sliding off.

They caught up with Sue around the next corner. She was on her phone, which surprised Kate because cell service was notoriously unreliable on the mountain. Most of the time, you couldn't even get one bar.

"What's up?" Brad said, skidding to a stop beside his sister.

Kate wished she could do that. Just stop, whenever she wanted. She tried to copy Brad's maneuver and fell over again. This time, she burst out laughing. So did Brad and Sue. Their giggles echoed eerily in the narrow ravine.

"One of Dad's instructors has called in sick," Sue said. "He needs me to teach a lesson."

"Now?" Brad said, helping Kate get up for a second time.

His sister nodded. "The three-year-olds."

"Oh, fun," Kate said. "Those kids on the bunny slope are totally amazing. They're all over the place."

"Tell me about it," Sue said. "It's worse than herding kittens." With a rueful grin, she pocketed her phone. "So, can you guys manage to stay out of trouble without me?"

"We'll do our best," Brad said.

Sue stuck out her tongue, then flashed off down the trail. Within seconds, she was out of sight. Brad said she'd be back at the lodge in five minutes by taking a black diamond short cut.

"Which one?" Kate said.

"*Jaws of Death.*"

Its name gave Kate the creeps. "Will she be okay?"

"Sue's been skiing that trail since she was a toddler," Brad said.

Astonished, Kate looked at him.

"She went down *Jaws* before I did," Brad said. "In my dad's backpack."

"Really?" Kate said.

Brad grinned. "Yes, really. Two years later, Sue did it by herself. She was probably the youngest kid ever to ski all the way from the top to the bottom without stopping." He paused to tighten his boots. "But she was so bundled up you couldn't tell if she was standing upright or sliding on her backside."

"Did you watch her?"

Brad nodded. "And my mom took videos."

It was common knowledge around the barn that Sue was a seriously good ski racer. Last season, she beat Angela in the downhill and came a close second in the giant slalom against a group of older skiers. With Jennifer now winning most of the club's junior tennis tournaments and Kate collecting blue ribbons in the show ring, Holly predicted that Mrs. Dean would have to find another sport for Angela to win at . . . or find her another horse.

Kate had forgotten all about Skywalker and City Woman. She'd even forgotten about Mrs. Gordon fussing over her father's books at the museum, dusting them with reverent care as though they were priceless relics. Up here in the mountain's silent world of deep snow and frozen waterfalls it was easy to believe that the rest of civilization was a million miles away. A gentle breeze picked up and ruffled a pine tree loaded with icicles. They tinkled like a hundred tiny bells.

"C'mon," Brad said. "You're daydreaming."

Pulling her scattered thoughts together, Kate concentrated on following Brad as he did a modified snowplow down the narrow trail. She turned when he turned, making sure not to ride up the snow banks on either side and get stuck. Bit by bit, she felt her skis coming together. They were almost parallel.

"You're doing great," Brad yelled.

He skied a little further on and stopped at the edge to watch her. Leaning forward, Kate bent her knees and speeded up. It felt as if she were floating on air, effortless and graceful, and—

Omigod, the snow bank!

Desperately, Kate jerked her skis to avoid Brad, but she crashed into him anyway and they both went flying in a jumble of arms, legs, and skis. The brakes on their bindings jammed together and it took Brad a few moments to unlock them. To keep from staring at his face, Kate concentrated on the orange zigzags that ran all over his jacket like bolts of lightning. Finally, the bindings broke loose.

"Yea!" Brad said and gave Kate a triumphant fist bump. Then he grabbed her hand and squeezed it, kind of hard.

She pulled away. "Ouch."

"Sorry," he said. "I guess I don't know my own strength."

"Tell that to Magician," Kate said, trying to make a joke. It seemed like no matter how she reacted with Brad, it always came out wrong. Her hand tingled inside its mitten. Kate couldn't tell if it was a good tingle or a bad one.

Brad said, "There's a plus side to all this."

"There is?" Kate said. "What?"

"You're learning how to fall."

"Yeah, right," she said. "But I'm not learning how to get up again."

That was the hard part, and Kate had a sinking feeling that maybe she wasn't cut out to be a skier. To her surprise, neither was Holly. She'd claimed it was because she had two left feet, which was kind of crazy given how brilliant she was at riding and swimming. Nobody could beat her in the butterfly, thanks to all the time she'd spent in the pool when she was confined to her wheelchair and swimming laps was her only exercise.

Determined to do it by herself, Kate managed to stand up without Brad's help. He retrieved her poles and gave them to her.

"Ready for more?" he said.

Kate gritted her teeth. Somehow, she would do this. She would *not* give up—at least, not till she got to the bottom of the hill. But first, she wanted to watch Brad in the half-pipe. She'd never seen it for real—just on TV at the last Winter Olympics when a kid with flying red hair became a snowboarding heartthrob.

*　*　*

Brad flipped, twisted, and soared like a sky diver. His amazing stunts had peculiar names like "Frontside Shifty" and "Double McTwist," and they left Kate with her mouth hanging open. She could barely watch—it looked so dangerous.

Jennifer sighed. "I wish I could do that."

"You can," Adam said, swooshing up to join them. "Get Brad to teach you."

"Where's Holly?" Kate said.

Her best friend had planned to ride the chairlift up to the half-pipe with Adam and ride it back down again when they were through watching the snowboarders, but there was no sign of her—just Jennifer and Robin and a bunch of girls from school who were all agog over Brad.

"Mucking stalls," Adam said.

Kate couldn't help herself. She felt instantly guilty for finking out on barn chores. Liz had taken Aunt Bea to a dressage clinic and everyone else was skiing which meant Holly was on her own. She probably didn't care, but Kate did.

"I'm going back," she said to Adam.

"Why?"

"Because I've had enough."

Kate's thigh muscles were burning and she couldn't wait to take her ski boots off. Stomping around in riding boots would be a breeze after this.

"Do you know the way?" Adam said.

She patted her pocket. "I've got a map."

"Okay," he said. "But hurry. It's gonna snow."

Kate had been so busy watching Brad that she hadn't noticed the clouds. The blue sky they'd started out with earlier had now turned a menacing shade of gray, the same color as Adam's jacket.

He said, "Should I come with you?"

"Thanks, but I'll be fine," Kate said.

She felt guilty enough about Holly coping with barn chores on her own, never mind how she'd feel if Adam gave up his snowboarding lesson with Brad. She shot him a confident smile and skied off. The hunt course was nearby. As soon as she found it, she'd know exactly where she was.

6

Twenty minutes later, Kate plowed to a stop. She'd ridden these trails many times with Holly, but they looked totally different under five feet of snow. There was an odd, muffled silence broken only by overhead cables that clanked and whined as they carried the gondola cars upward. Familiar landmarks had disappeared. Kate searched her pockets for the trail map and came up empty.

Where was it?

Snow began to fall. Flakes the size of cottonballs landed on her sunglasses. She tried to wipe them off with her mittens but ended up smearing them instead. Kate ransacked her pockets again and realized that her map must've fallen out.

Okay. Don't panic.

There'd be a map posted somewhere. She'd seen them before—huge yellow bulletin boards at trail junctions that were hard to miss. With luck, they'd tell her where she was.

The wind picked up. It sliced into Kate's nose and ran its cold fingers down her cheeks as she skied cautiously along the winding trail. Was the hunt course ahead or behind her? Was it even in this direction? She couldn't tell any more.

After what seemed like hours but was probably only a few minutes, the trail forked. Snow had obliterated the signs and their metal posts were bent like pretzels as if someone had laid into them with a sledgehammer. Reaching up, Kate wiped off enough snow to make out the words. One was a blue trail called *Dreamweaver*; the other was a black diamond. Its name, *Nightmare*, gave her the shivers.

No sign of a big trail map, either.

For a couple of frozen moments, Kate stared at the twisted signs. Not a green trail in sight, so what had gone wrong? Had she missed a turning? Easy to do in this bad weather. The snow was coming down even faster now.

Kate read the signs again. *Dreamweaver* didn't sound too bad. She'd never skied a blue trail before. Brad said most of them weren't that much more difficult than the green ones.

Besides, she didn't have many choices, other than to take her skis off and hike back up the hill to where she'd started out or to call the ski patrol.

Brad had told her about that as well.

Special phones in red waterproof boxes were scattered all over Timber Ridge. If you needed help, you just opened the box and called. The ski patrol had sleds with blankets and first-aid kits and would take you down the mountain to safety.

Was there a red box here?

Kate looked around, but she didn't see one. Not that she'd use it. She'd be way too embarrassed to show up at the base lodge strapped to a sled unless she was injured, which she wasn't. She was just a little bit scared.

No. Make that a *lot* scared.

With no other option, Kate followed the blue sign and headed for *Dreamweaver*. According to Brad, blue trails were well groomed and didn't have moguls, unless the bump skiers had mashed them into mounds on purpose.

"They're responsible for the moguls," he'd said. "Not us. We don't bury old Volkswagens. That's an urban legend."

Urban legend or not, this blue trail had a whole rack

of moguls, sticking up like giant eggs in a carton. Some really were the size of Volkswagens. Swallowing hard, Kate gripped her poles as other skiers whizzed past, curving around the bumps at high speed. A couple of them yelled at her.

"Heads up," they cried. "On your right."

Kate understood. Athletes all over used the same words. She'd shouted them herself when out riding and jumping the cross-country course. The last thing you wanted was a hapless beginner getting in your way. She risked a quick glance down the slope.

Not a good idea.

It was way steeper than she imagined—kind of like looking at jumps from the ground and then looking at them again from the back of a horse, where they suddenly looked a whole lot higher. Legs trembling, Kate began to inch her way down.

This wasn't a dream, it was a nightmare.

* * *

Holly finished sweeping the aisle and checked her watch. It was almost three. Kate should be back by now. She wasn't a good enough skier to stay out all day with the others.

A tickle of worry ran down Holly's spine.

Best to ignore it. Kate would be fine. She wouldn't go

off skiing by herself without Brad or Sue. If anything had gone wrong, they'd be all over it and Holly's cell phone would be hammered with text messages.

But it wasn't.

There was just one from Mom and another from Adam, who said he'd be back around four-thirty. Holly hit the button to make sure her phone was connected. It rang within seconds.

She almost dropped it. "Hello?"

"Hi, it's me," came Adam's voice. "Did Kate get back yet?"

"No," Holly said. "Is she okay?"

"I don't know," he said. "She took off about half an hour ago, and I've tried calling her, but—"

The connection ended abruptly, the way it always did from the mountain. Angrily, Holly shook her cell phone as if that would jump-start it into action. But it remained stubbornly mute.

Okay, so half an hour.

It took longer than that to ride a horse back down from the half-pipe, so it would probably take Kate even longer, given she was a brand new skier. But this was just a guess. Holly knew as much about skiing as she knew about particle physics and linear equations.

Hanging up her broom, Holly made for the tack room. She pulled Magician's saddle off its peg, then gathered up her currycomb, hoof pick, and brushes. Mom wasn't too keen on people riding alone when there was nobody else in the barn, but Magician needed schooling. Kate would be way too stiff to get any riding done today, so Holly would do it for her.

Besides, she hadn't ridden her own horse in over a week.

* * *

Somehow, without killing herself or anyone else, Kate snow-plowed around the first line of moguls and stumbled to safety on the trail's other side. Pine trees, twisted into odd shapes by the wind, towered above her. Awkwardly, she turned around and skied back, narrowly missing a couple of kids who zoomed over the bumps like exuberant puppies let loose from a cage.

The onslaught of skiers tapered off and Kate found herself alone—trapped between an impenetrable forest on one side and a never-ending sea of moguls on the other. Unwilling to risk another trip across the slope, Kate pulled out her cell and punched in Adam's number. Maybe it would work this time.

He answered on the first ring. "Where *are* you?"

"*Dreamweaver*," Kate said.

In the background, she heard the unmistakable scrape and swish of snowboards, followed by Adam talking to Brad, probably about the slope she was stranded on. Adam didn't know them nearly as well as Brad did.

"Hang in there," Adam said. "We'll come and find you."

"With a sled?" Kate had visions of half the ski patrol showing up and turning her dumb mistake into a three-ring circus. This was all her fault. If she'd paid more attention to the trail signs or hadn't lost her map, she wouldn't be stuck on a hill with moguls big enough to scare the living daylights out of a mountain goat.

Adam laughed. "No, but Brad says he'll give you a piggyback to the bottom if you want."

Even though both cheeks were numb with cold, Kate felt herself blush. She hung up and checked the time. Adam and Brad skied like maniacs. It wouldn't take them long to reach her—maybe ten minutes, fifteen at the most.

* * *

Dusk crept down the mountain like a panther, stealthy and mysterious. Kate could barely see the other side of the trail. Only the moguls stood out, glistening with ice where skiers had rubbed them raw.

Maybe the ski patrol would come by.

If they did, Kate would forget her embarrassment

and jump on whatever sled they offered. Or maybe they had come down and she'd missed them. Brad said they checked all the slopes after the last lift had closed to make sure nobody got stuck on the mountain all night.

Out of the gloom, two skiers appeared, dodging and weaving among the bumps. They were too far away to make out clearly, but those orange flashes looked a whole lot like the ones on Brad's snowboarding jacket.

"Over here," Kate yelled.

"Stay where you are," came the reply.

But Kate couldn't wait. Filled with relief, she pushed off the bank and hit a patch of ice. Her skis began to slide apart, as if she were doing splits. Frantically, she tried to pull them together but her tired legs refused to cooperate. One ski binding released; the other didn't and it corkscrewed Kate into a twisting, slow-motion fall.

Pain exploded in her left knee.

Adam reached her first. He bent to pull her up but Brad stopped him. "Don't move her."

In a blur of pain, Kate could see that Brad was on his cell—miraculously working—and kneeling beside her as he called for help. "We're at the head of *Nightmare*," he said. "On the right, about two hundred yards down."

Nightmare?

"The sled'll be here in a few minutes," Brad told

Kate, keeping a steady hand on her shoulder. "Hold still, okay?"

She didn't have much choice.

Her knee hurt way too much to even think about moving or getting up. A bazillion stupid thoughts raced through her mind with dizzying speed, like going to school on crutches and not being able to help her father at the museum. And what about the qualifying show? It was in less than four weeks and there wasn't another before the Festival of Horses. If she didn't make this one, she was totally cooked.

7

MUCH TO KATE'S EMBARRASSMENT, the ski patrol brought her off the mountain. Brad skied alongside the sled, hovering beside it like an anxious mother hen while Kate lay flat out, held down by straps and unable to move.

By the time they reached the Timber Ridge medical unit, Adam had alerted the troops. Liz left a message saying that Holly's orthopedic surgeon would meet them at the hospital's ER.

"It's nothing," Kate protested.

Brad released her from the sled. "Hush."

Politely, he turned his back while a medic with gentle hands peeled off Kate's snow pants and long underwear, but all Kate could think about was her hairy legs. She hadn't shaved them since before Christmas.

"Not important," Holly whispered.

When had she shown up?

Woozy with pain, Kate vaguely registered a trip in the ambulance. Sirens wailed and lights flashed as they pulled into the same hospital where she'd taken Holly after the fire that destroyed a small barn at Timber Ridge and forced her best friend to walk again.

* * *

"You've torn your MCL," declared the doctor, looking at Kate's X-rays on a screen beside her bed.

"What's that?" Kate said. Her knee didn't hurt any more, but that was because they'd shot it full of painkillers.

"Medial collateral ligament," Holly said.

Her doctor nodded. "I figured you'd know what that was."

But Kate didn't. Not until the doctor showed her a diagram of the knee and all the bits and pieces it contained. It was like looking at something in biology class, only worse. This was *her* knee, not a dead frog she was about to dissect.

The hospital curtains parted and there was her father. His tie was askew, his shirt buttoned up all wrong. He reached for Kate's hand and held onto it like a lifeline. "Are you okay?" he said. Behind him came Mrs. Gordon.

Kate grimaced. "Yeah, Dad. I'm all right."

Nurses bustled in and out of Kate's cubicle. Machines bleeped, lights blinked, and an EKG monitored Kate's heart rate with a needle that scribbled up and down like an Excel graph gone berserk. She wanted to throw herself into Dad's arms, but not in front of The Gorgon.

Holly's ortho-doc gave Kate her verdict. "Ice and rest for three days," she said. "After that, you can begin exercising with a brace. Swimming is good, but nothing too strenuous. Let pain be your guide. When it hurts, stop."

"How long will it take?" Kate said.

"Four weeks," replied the doc. "Maybe longer, but it's hard to tell. Some people heal faster than others." She looked at her clipboard. "It says here that you ride horses, yes?"

Kate nodded.

The doc shook her head. "None of that till the end of January. Your MCL is only a first-level tear, but if that knee gets stressed, it'll get worse." She scribbled something on a piece of paper and gave it to Kate. "Make an appointment with a physical therapist, and I'll see you in mid-February."

Her pager buzzed.

She pulled it from her belt, frowned, then left the cubicle to visit her next patient—probably that kid Kate had seen in the waiting room who had a cast on both arms. He had it a whole lot worse than Kate did. At least she'd be able to eat without help and brush her own teeth.

* * *

Kate's father drove Holly home, then dropped off Mrs. Gordon before taking Kate and her crutches back to their cottage. It was way beyond dinner but Kate wasn't hungry. She hadn't even had any lunch, unless you counted the energy bar Brad had shared with her before they hit the half-pipe.

Dad heated up a can of vegetable soup, slapped together a tuna sandwich, and more or less forced her to eat. "Your knee won't heal if you starve it to death," he said.

Listlessly, Kate picked at her sandwich. She swallowed two spoonfuls of soup and pushed it away. How could she eat when the doctor had just trashed her one and only shot at The Festival of Horses?

* * *

Late the following afternoon, Brad solved the puzzle of why Kate had ended up on *Nightmare*. He stuck his head around the tack room door as Kate was cleaning bridles, slumped in a saggy old armchair with her leg propped on a pile of sheepskins and horse blankets. Dad had wanted her to stay home, but Kate convinced him she'd go completely nuts if she was stuck in the cottage with nothing to do but sit around feeling sorry for herself.

"How's it going?" Brad bent over Kate's knee.

She shifted uncomfortably. " 'S okay."

Her ice pack had pretty much melted. There were two more in the tack room's tiny freezer. Holly had made sure of that before racing off to handle barn chores and help her mom with lessons. They'd already commiserated with Kate over missing the show.

"Maybe it'll get better in time," Holly had said, sounding hopeful. But Liz shook her head. She'd pulled a tendon the previous summer and had been unable to ride for at least a month.

Brad replaced Kate's ice pack, then unfolded a metal chair and sat on it backward, facing Kate with his arms crossed and his chin resting on top. She gulped. It was a bit unnerving, trying not to stare at an awesomely cute guy whose eyes were the same color as yours—mossy green with flecks of gold which some people called hazel.

"The trail signs got messed up," Brad said.

Kate pulled herself together. "How?"

"One of our snow-grooming machines banged into

them," he said. "The signs fell off, and the driver put them back up again, but switched them by mistake." There was a pause. "I'm sorry, really sorry."

"So, I didn't flub up?"

"Nope," Brad said. "We did."

It was good to hear, but it didn't help. Kate was grounded for a month, maybe longer. Earlier that morning the physical therapist had coached her through a series of leg exercises, some of which Kate recognized from helping Holly when she was still stuck in her wheelchair. None of them had worked for Holly because the paralysis had been all in her head. But Kate's injury wasn't. Her knee was a hot mess, and—

Holly skidded into the tack room. "Mom needs a longer girth for Daisy, but—" She stared at Kate, then transferred her steely gaze to Brad. "What's going on?"

He explained about the trail signs.

"Yikes," Holly said. "Good thing Angela's not here."

"Why?" Brad said, looking puzzled.

He wasn't privy to barn politics. According to Holly, guys couldn't see beyond Angela's fluttering lashes, pale blue eyes, and those pouty lips that hid a venomous tongue she'd never dream of using on them.

"Because this is exactly what *she'd* do," Holly said, striking a dramatic pose. She winked at Brad and blew him a movie-star kiss. "But this time, Princess Angela's in the clear—unless she hired a hitman all the way from Colorado."

Despite herself, Kate burst out laughing.

The first time she'd competed against Angela was at a three-day event. They were the last two riders on the cross-country course, and Angela—who went right before Kate—managed to destroy half the markers. Kate had gotten lost and galloped over the finish line with just a few seconds left on the clock.

* * *

Brad's father insisted on buying Kate a two-month membership at the Timber Ridge fitness center. It had an indoor pool, a therapeutic hot tub, and exercise machines with all the latest bells and whistles. "It's the least we can do," Brad said when Kate protested that the school gym was good enough.

"Take it," Holly said after Brad left. "And you can move back in with us. You'll be a lot closer to the club and you won't have to mess with those awful stairs at the cottage."

"Will your mom mind?"

"Don't be stupid," Holly said. "She'll love it."

"Thanks." Kate heaved a sigh of relief.

She'd had a rough time that morning, getting down Aunt Marion's narrow staircase. Being at Holly's would be a whole lot easier. Her house was all one floor. There was even a ramp at the front door, left over from when Holly was in a wheelchair. Liz hadn't gotten around to taking it down.

"Uh, oh," Holly said.

Kate looked at her. "What?"

"This means leaving your dad *alone* with The Gorgon," Holly said, pulling a face.

Kate hadn't even thought of that. "But he's with her all day, at the museum."

"I know," Holly said, "but this would be *after* work. Without you there, she'd just casually drop by to make sure he's okay and has enough to eat, and the next thing you know they'd be opening a bottle of wine, and—"

"*Stop!*" Kate covered both ears. "That's crazy."

But was it? Ever since Mrs. Gordon showed up at the barn with her father and then at Holly's house on Christmas Day, Kate had begun to worry. Maybe the cooking lessons for Liz and her dad wouldn't be enough to jump-start the romance that Holly insisted was already there. The trouble was that her father wouldn't recognize a romance unless it fluttered past him on four wings.

"Know what we need?" Holly said.

"Magic?" Kate said. "Fairy dust?"

"Close," Holly said. "We need Mary Poppins and Nanny McPhee, all rolled into one."

Kate rubbed her chin. "I'm growing a wart."

"That's backward," Holly said, giggling. "They're supposed to disappear." She narrowed her eyes. "Maybe we could make Mrs. Gordon disappear."

"Like, how?"

"I dunno," Holly said. "I need to work on it."

* * *

On New Year's Day, a flashy gold-and-black rig with Virginia license plates pulled into the barn's parking lot. Holly had been working Magician over fences and she'd just finished cooling him off when everyone rushed outside. She threw a blanket on her horse, fed him a carrot, and followed the crowd. Behind her, Kate limped along on her crutches.

"Hey, wait up," she cried.

Holly stopped because she knew exactly how it felt to be left out. For two years, she'd trundled along in her wheelchair—always behind the other kids, always late for whatever was going on because she'd gotten stuck in a narrow doorway or had confronted some steps that forced her to make a detour.

Then there were the birthday parties she wasn't invited to because nobody could figure out how to get her—and the bulky wheelchair—into their homes without calling the Fire Department for help.

"You okay?" she said to Kate.

Her best friend winced. "Yeah."

When they joined the other girls, Holly whistled through her teeth. Mom hadn't said a word about this. She was still in her office with the door shut and probably didn't realize that everyone was outside gawking at the unexpected arrival.

Holly had seen vans like this before.

They showed up at big events like Devon and Kentucky-Rolex, complete with security cameras, flush toilets, and queen-size beds—sometimes, even a jacuzzi. This rig probably cost a half million dollars.

Out of the driver's cab stepped a man wearing field boots, buff breeches, and a black parka with gold trim. Another, dressed exactly the same, marched to the rear of the van and unhitched the ramp. Both men wore *ushankas*—those funny-looking hats with ear flaps that Holly had learned about in social studies—and she half expected them to click their heels and salute like Russian soldiers.

"Who *is* this?" Robin said.

Jennifer grinned. "The royals?"

There was no name on the van—just a small gold

crest on both sides. Its wheels had gold-colored hubcaps, and even the bumpers shone. No sign of any salt or mud, either. Maybe they'd run it through the local car wash before showing up here. If so, the horse inside had to be going ballistic right about now.

But it wasn't.

At a nod from the driver, the other man lowered the van's ramp and the horse backed out—ears pricked, nostrils gently flaring, but completely at home as if he already owned every inch of Timber Ridge.

8

KATE COULDN'T TAKE HER EYES off the new horse. He demanded attention. His dark bay coat gleamed like well-polished mahogany; his nose and ears shone as if someone had rubbed them with Vaseline. Even his feet glittered. They sparkled like a movie star's engagement ring.

"He's got bling," Holly cried. "Look."

"Way cool," Jennifer said.

Leaning on both crutches, Kate rubbed her eyes and looked again. Sure enough, silver baubles studded the gelding's flashy hooves. She'd seen photos of this on Facebook but figured it had to be a joke. Horses with fancy manicures? No way.

"I want one," Sue said.

"A new horse?" said Robin.

Sue waggled her fingers. "New nails."

"Then stop biting them," Robin said, giving her best friend a sharp nudge. Sue scowled and shoved both hands in her pockets.

Just then, the barn door opened and Liz strode out. She conferred with the van's driver, signed his paperwork, and took hold of the gelding's black-and-gold lead rope.

"Angela's new horse?" Kate said.

Holly nodded. "It must be," she said. "Who else can afford a Dutch Warmblood with diamonds on its feet?"

* * *

Holly had guessed right about the breed. Angela's new horse was a ten-year-old Warmblood and he'd already proved himself a winner on the three-day-event circuit.

In an odd way, he looked comfortingly familiar, nibbling bits of grain from Skywalker's feed bucket. It was as if Angela had swapped her old horse for a replica, except this one was three inches taller and carried a lot more muscle. Someone, probably Liz, had replaced the stall's brass nameplate.

Ragtime, said the new one.

"Awesome name," Jennifer said, running her hands down the newcomer's velvety nose. He whickered softly and nudged her pocket for treats. She pulled out a carrot.

"Scot Joplin," Holly muttered.

Kate looked at her. "Who?"

"The King of Ragtime," Holly said and did a bouncy little two-step down the aisle.

Trust Holly to know that. She adored old music the same way she adored old movies. At the tack room door, she turned and danced back. Nobody would ever know she'd once been paralyzed from the waist down. Kate shifted on her crutches. They were just about the most uncomfortable things she'd ever had to deal with—worse than the braces she'd worn on her teeth in seventh grade.

"Where did they find him?" Jennifer said, feeding Ragtime another carrot. "Horses like this don't grow on trees."

Liz said, "Mrs. Dean hired a buyer's agent."

"A what?" Holly said.

"Someone who helps you find the perfect horse," her mother replied. "For a fee."

"Like a commission?" Kate said. She'd heard of this before. A well-known dressage rider who'd recently re-tired from the show ring was reported as earning twenty percent on every deal he brokered. "Who was the agent?"

"Lockie Malone," Liz said, consulting her notes. "It says here that he's from a private barn in Connecticut."

She glanced at Kate. "Maybe your old riding teacher knows him."

The name rang a few distant bells, but Kate couldn't put her finger on them. She ransacked her memory and came up with nothing except an odd feeling she'd heard that name before.

Holly said, "Look him up."

While the others made a fuss of Ragtime, Kate did a quick search on her cell phone. She tried different spellings and found herself on a web page about the Loch Ness monster. As she flipped through screens, Kate began to wonder if Angela had actually ridden her expensive new horse. She hadn't said a word about it, which was really weird. Angela never missed an opportunity to show off.

"You know what this means," Holly whispered.

Startled, Kate looked up. "What?"

"Angela's going to ace the next show," Holly said, sounding grim. "And she'll have the team scouts crawling all over her at the Festival."

"Don't be silly," Kate said. "You'll beat her."

"So will you."

Kate sighed. Never mind what the doctor said, Holly was absolutely convinced that Kate's knee would heal in time for her to compete at the end of January. But was it worth the pain and effort? With Angela's new horse, all the goalposts had moved. Nobody, not even Liz, could predict what would happen next.

* * *

The second day of school was half over by the time Angela showed up with Kristina James. Their tanned faces and perpetual sneers hit Kate the minute she hobbled into the cafeteria.

"Nice crutches," Angela said.

Kristina giggled. "Pity they don't match your outfit."

She was Angela's newest best friend in a long line of best friends who'd fallen by the wayside. Like a stand-up comedian, Angela needed an obedient sidekick who'd always laugh at her jokes. She wasn't allowed to outshine Angela in the looks department, either.

Kristina fit the bill perfectly.

She had chestnut brown hair—not nearly as dramatic as Angela's flowing black mane—and light-brown eyes that faded to insignificance beside Angela's icy blue ones, which drilled holes into anyone brave enough to stare at her long enough.

"Ignore them," Holly said.

Brad stuck out his foot, hooked an empty chair, and pulled it over to their table. "Sit with us," he said, snagging another so that Kate could put her leg up.

Gratefully, she dumped her tray and sat down. Getting around school on crutches, not being late for class, and carrying her books was a major challenge. She'd dropped them outside the school office that morning and the vice principal had helped pick them up. He'd suggested that Kate get a suitcase on wheels.

"And how does he think I'll pull it?" Kate had grumbled to Holly when they connected in homeroom. "With my teeth?"

"No, a harness," Holy replied.

More kids joined their lunch table. Amid arguments about the basketball team's chances against the neighboring high school and a substitute teacher's horrible biology quiz, they tucked into garden salads, sausage pizza, and chocolate pudding. Jennifer whispered in Kate's ear.

"Meet us at the barn after school."

"Okay, sure." Kate bent to adjust the Velcro straps on her knee brace. "After I get done with my daily torture."

She'd already pushed herself through four rigorous sessions at the Timber Ridge club, pounding the exercise machines and swimming laps. Brad insisted on driving her. He'd hung about, talking on his cell and doing his homework, and had then driven her back to the barn or to Holly's house. It was kind of nice but a bit embarrassing, the way he fussed over her. Guilt, probably. No doubt his father had made him do it.

"No," Jennifer said. "Come before."

She shot Kate a knowing look and then glanced toward the end table where Angela sat with Kristina, her cousin Courtney, and the cheerleading squad. They all wore matching outfits—green tops that barely covered their midriffs and short green skirts with yellow stripes. And even though they all seemed to be talking at once, Angela's voice, shrill and demanding, rose above the others.

"Why?" Kate said.

Jennifer leaned closer. "To watch Angela ride."

* * *

Liz had already ridden Ragtime, but Kate missed it. According to the other girls, Angela's new horse had performed multiple flying changes, a flawless half pass, and an extended trot to die for.

"What about jumping?" Kate said.

Sue gave a big sigh. "Brilliant."

"Totally," Robin said, nodding so vigorously that her dark-brown curls bounced about like demented Slinkies.

Ragtime was also bombproof. Nothing fazed him—not even the barn's two feral cats that streaked down the aisle and zoomed beneath his feet like furry missiles. All he did was curl his upper lip, as if he were laughing.

"Amazing, huh?" Jennifer said.

At a loss for words, Kate just nodded as Holly led the big bay gelding back into his stall. When Mother Nature was handing out favors, Ragtime got more than his fair share—stunning good looks, athletic prowess, and the unflappability of a highly trained police horse. He probably cost more than the van he arrived in.

Behind her, Tapestry whickered.

Kate turned, almost tripping over her crutches. Awkwardly, she slid open the stall door. Tapestry snorted. She still wasn't too sure about the crutches and gave them a wary look.

"They won't hurt you," Kate said, wincing. "They only hurt me." Her underarms were sore, aching more than her knee did. Next week the physical therapist said she'd be ready to graduate from crutches to canes, and Kate couldn't wait.

Propping her crutches outside Tapestry's stall, Kate hobbled inside. It was hard to believe, but she hadn't ridden Tapestry for almost three weeks. She'd been riding Magician instead, and now—thanks to her own stupidity—she wasn't riding either one of them.

Kate held out a carrot. "Come on, girl."

Tapestry whickered again. She took a step toward Kate, then hesitated before whuffling up the treat. Kate wrapped both arms around her mare's warm golden neck and hung on as tight as she could. Tears pricked her eyelids. Kate tried to fight them, but they escaped anyway. One rolled down her cheek, then another. They landed in Tapestry's silvery mane and glistened, just for a moment, like the jewels on Ragtime's feet.

Get a grip, Kate told herself.

This wasn't the end of the world. She *would* survive, the way she'd survived being wrongly blamed for a horse's death at her old barn in Connecticut and Angela's attempts to sabotage her reputation at Timber Ridge. More than once, she'd accused Kate of cheating.

Behind her, Holly said, "She's here."

"Who?" Kate sniffed, but didn't turn.

Holly put a hand on Kate's shoulder. "Angela," she said. "Hey, are you okay?"

"Yes," Kate said. "I'm fine."

"Liar," Holly said, and thrust a crumpled tissue at her. "Look, I know you think I'm nuts, but I bet you'll be okay to ride. Think about Nicole Hoffman. She broke her collar bone and won a gold medal the next day. Remember?"

Kate blew her nose, feeling like a wimp.

Nicole Hoffman was one of her favorite stars. She'd trained at Beaumont Park, a world-class equestrian center in England. It was owned by Jennifer West's grandmother, who'd invited Holly and Kate to train there next summer at a special camp for teen riders.

There was a noise in the aisle.

"Heads up," Holly whispered, and propelled Kate toward the door. "Barbie Dolls on parade."

Leaning on both crutches, Kate stifled her giggles as Angela, flanked by Courtney and Kristina, strutted toward them like models from a teenage sports magazine. Angela and Kristina were dressed in skintight breeches, Ariat boots, and fur-trimmed vests. Courtney was wearing a neon-pink tennis dress and matching wristbands that were so bright they made Kate blink.

Holly whipped out her sunglasses. "That's better," she said. "Now I can see."

With her pert little nose in the air, Angela swept past. She headed straight for her horse's stall. Ears pricked as if he sensed more lavish attention, Ragtime stuck his head over the door and whickered.

Angela froze. "What's *that* horse doing in *my* stall?"

"Uh, oh," Holly said. "I smell trouble."

Eyes blazing like beacons, Angela whipped around. "What's going on here? Where's Skywalker?"

TIME STOOD STILL. The barn fell silent as everyone stared at Angela. Her expression ran the gamut from disbelief to white-faced anger. For a few confused moments, Kate felt desperately sorry for her. Didn't Angela know about this? Had her mother sold Skywalker and bought another horse without telling her?

"Liz," Angela yelled.

Holly's mother emerged from the tack room. From the puzzled look on her face, it was obvious she didn't know about Mrs. Dean's tactics either. She paused in mid-stride, as if assessing the situation, then led a tearful Angela into her office and shut the door. Its abrupt click sent a strong message.

No interruptions.

Jennifer cleared her throat. "So, who's gonna ride?"

"I will," Robin said.

Holly nodded. "Me, too."

Then Sue chimed in—and so did Kristina. Quietly, she slipped into Cody's stall and hugged him, which surprised Kate. Angela's best friend had been at Timber Ridge for a month, but this was the first time Kate had ever seen Kristina show affection for her gorgeous palomino.

While the others groomed and tacked up their horses, Kate sat on a hay bale, deep in thought. She'd expected the barn to explode with rumors and wild speculation, the way it had when Skywalker left. Yet nobody, it seemed, was ready to talk about why Angela didn't recognize her new horse. They were probably putting themselves in Angela's shoes and hating the way it felt.

But one thing was painfully clear.

Mrs. Dean had blindsided her own daughter. No matter how selfish and mean Angela was, she didn't deserve this. Kate let out a ragged sigh. Mothers were supposed to support their children—not throw them under the bus.

The only one not bothered by Mrs. Dean's treachery was Courtney. She scooped her blond hair into a ponytail, secured it with a neon-pink scrunchie, and sashayed off, swinging her designer tennis racquet as if she didn't have a care in the world.

"See ya," she said and sauntered out.

* * *

Kate spent the next hour in the arena's observation room watching her team in action and wishing for the millionth time that she was out there with them, riding Magician or Tapestry or even lazy old Daisy. It didn't matter, as long as she was on a horse instead of stuck in a metal chair.

When they got back into the barn, Liz's office door was wide open and Angela had disappeared. There was no sign of Liz, either. Ragtime stood in his stall, leaning out and whickering hopefully at anyone who walked past.

"Love bunny," Holly said, patting him.

Kate fed him her last carrot. "I feel kind of bad for Angela."

"I don't," Holly said, sounding fierce. "She didn't give a hoot about Skywalker, and she won't care about Ragtime either. The only thing that bothered her was looking stupid in front of us."

"Yes, but—" Kate started to say, and then Brad ambled up. Probably a good thing, too. He'd inadvertently stopped her from defending Angela when she wasn't even sure why she was doing it.

"You ready for the club?" he said.

Kate nodded. "In a few minutes."

She left Holly trying to give Brad the lowdown on

what had just happened with Angela and limped into Tapestry's stall. This time, the mare didn't bat an eyelash over Kate's crutches. As Kate leaned into Tapestry's warmth, she decided to ask Jennifer or maybe Robin if they'd have time to exercise her. Holly had her hands full with Magician because she refused to give up on the idea of Kate competing and wanted her horse to be in tip-top shape.

Kate looked down at her knee.

Friends had scrawled cartoons and funny messages all over her brace. You could hardly tell what color it had once been. With a glittery pink pen, Holly had drawn the Nike swoosh. Beneath it, she'd written *Just Do It*.

* * *

A gaudy mural—lime-green palm trees, silvery sand, and a turquoise lagoon—covered the spa's far wall. Chaises and bistro tables sat in front of a picture window frosted with snow; fake vines climbed unconvincingly up the poles of grass umbrellas. Or maybe they were plastic done up to look like grass.

Kate couldn't tell.

Her eyes were raw from swimming. Someone had over-chlorinated the pool again. Its smell hung in the air like a failed chemistry experiment. Another five minutes and she would get out. Her muscles ached, but in a good way. The physical therapist said that water resistance was perfect for retraining damaged ligaments. And it seemed to be working.

Already, Kate's knee was feeling better.

She glanced at Brad, slouched at a bistro table and frowning over his math quiz. He was in tenth grade, a year ahead of Kate and Holly, and he struggled with algebra. Kate had offered to help, but Brad resisted. Despite his kindness and common sense, he still bought into the myth that guys were supposed to be mathematical wizards and girls weren't.

It cut both ways. Kate loved math, but Holly didn't. Holly had a solid grasp of English and was a total genius when it came to Photoshop, and this was perfect because she wanted a career in graphic arts. But Kate planned to be a veterinarian—or maybe a doctor—and math was critical. So was chemistry.

Wrinkling her nose, Kate forced herself to swim another lap. Halfway down the pool, she turned and saw Brad waving her cell phone. She'd left it on the table with her wallet, rather than leaving them in the changing room's unreliable lockers.

"What's up?" she yelled, treading water.

"You've got a call."

It was probably her dad. "Take a message."

"Okay."

At the deep end, Kate did a flip turn and swung into the butterfly, her best stroke. Dad loved it, too, but only because of its name. He'd once tried to swim it—arms and legs all over the place—and Kate had jumped in to save him because she thought he was drowning.

She grinned and caught a mouthful of water. The butterfly didn't do much for her legs, but it challenged her shoulders. Brad was big on shoulders. His were impressive, and Kate felt like showing hers off.

Breathing hard, she climbed out of the pool. Brad threw her a towel and then handed over her phone. "I think you'd better call him back."

"My dad?"

"Nathan," Brad said. "He didn't sound too thrilled at hearing my voice."

* * *

Kate tried to strap on her knee brace, but her fingers refused to cooperate. So Brad did it for her. Carefully, he jockeyed the brace back and forth until it settled into position. His gentle hands sent a soft tingle down her spine.

"Feel okay?" he said.

"Yes," Kate said. "And thanks."

Clutching her cell phone, she limped into the changing room and hit "redial," but her call ended up in

Nathan's voice mail. Okay, so how bad was this? On a scale of one to ten?

Maybe a five. Okay, a six.

Nathan didn't know about her friendship with Brad, and she hadn't told him because it was just a friendship.

Nothing more.

But some guys were really weird about stuff like this. They didn't get it that you could have a boy for a friend without it being romantic. It was a lost cause, trying to explain this to Nathan. He was in New Zealand where time zones and school schedules worked against you. Even emoticons didn't help. It wasn't easy to talk about tough stuff with your thumbs.

And as for talking in real time?

How did you wink at someone over the phone or let them know you were frowning? Kate tried calling Nathan once more—it was wickedly expensive to New Zealand—and didn't get through, so she fired off a text message instead.

Sorry. Missed your call. xxx Kate.

It sounded upbeat . . . but underneath it all, Kate was a mass of confusion. She didn't have a clue how to handle this, and having Sue's awesomely cute brother hovering over her made it even more complicated.

* * *

"Where to?" Brad asked, as they climbed into his truck. He took Kate's crutches and dumped them in the back seat.

"My dad's house," Kate said. "Is that okay?"

"Sure," he said, driving off.

She wanted to check on her father and comb through back issues of *Dressage Today*, *Chronicle of the Horse*, and *Young Rider*. One of them, she knew, would have information about Lockie Malone, the guy who'd helped Mrs. Dean buy Angela's new horse.

Brad offered to wait, but Kate said her father would drive her back to Holly's house. Or maybe she'd just spend the night in her own room, and—

Mrs. Gordon opened the front door.

"Kate," she said. "How nice to see you."

"What are *you* doing here?"

The words were out before Kate could stop them. Then Dad intervened, which was a good thing, otherwise she might've said something even ruder. Mrs. Gordon's face was already turning pale.

"I didn't expect you," he said.

Kate clumped inside. "Guess not."

There was a bottle of wine and two glasses on the coffee table. Holly was right. The Gorgon *was* trying to take over. Okay, how to cope with this? Pretend it didn't matter, or make a scene?

A thought crept into Kate's mind.

Something Holly said about making Mrs. Gordon disappear. Maybe if Kate acted like a spoiled brat, The Gorgon would give up and go home. It was childish and stupid, but worth a shot. Right now, Kate didn't have any other bright ideas.

But first she had to find Lockie Malone . . . if only to satisfy her own curiosity.

* * *

Stacks of old magazines sat in sliding piles on her bedroom floor. Kate had been meaning to put them on the top shelf in her closet and now was glad that she hadn't. Climbing onto a chair to get them would've been impossible with her knee. Just maneuvering herself up Aunt Marion's narrow stairs was bad enough. She hefted two piles onto her bed—back copies of *Dressage Today* and *Young Rider*—and began her search from the bottom.

It only took four issues.

She found his name and a photo in *Young Rider*, taken at the National Horse Show five years ago. It was hard to make out Lockie Malone's face beneath his helmet, but he looked kind of cute—tall and lean with a great tan. He was bending forward to receive a medal from a flashy blonde in sequins and ridiculously high heels.

Okay, so what happened next?

Did he go from juniors to the international show-jumping circuit? Sprawled across her bed, Kate flicked through the rest of her *Young Riders*, then ran through a year's worth of *Chronicle of the Horse* as well, but found nothing else about Lockie Malone. It was as if he disappeared from the face of the earth—just like Mrs. Gordon needed to do. Well, not disappear completely, but far enough away to leave Kate's father alone.

For a few moments, Kate sat on her bed, making faces at herself in the mirror above her vanity. She practiced scowling and sighing and rolling her eyes. She tried to look as bratty as possible. How about if she glowered and pretended to chew gum? No, that didn't work. Hauling herself upright, she put both hands on her hips and thrust them forward like the bullies at school did.

But that wasn't her style.

Besides, it wouldn't pass with a grownup who'd once been the high school principal. Mrs. Gordon was probably the world's expert on bratty behavior and knew exactly how to slap it down.

With a loud meow, Persy the kitten emerged from beneath Kate's bed and startled her. He was hardly a kitten at this point—more like a feline teenager with gangly legs and ears that were a little bit too large for his face.

Kate abandoned her theatrics, gathered up the cat,

and took him downstairs—one hand on the rail, the other wrapped around Persy while trying not to trip. She'd left her crutches propped against the couch. Behind them, Dad and Mrs. Gordon sat close—but not quite touching—as they sipped wine and flipped through Dad's latest butterfly book. Soft music wafted from the stereo; the lights were turned low. Kate wanted to throw up.

She parked Persy on the back of the couch and grabbed her crutches. The cat yawned and flexed his claws, stretching them out as if admiring an exotic new manicure. Then he sprang onto Mrs. Gordon's lap.

"Noooo!" she screamed.

Her glass flew in one direction, Dad's book in the other. It landed face down on the coffee table and sent the wine bottle skittering. Mrs. Gordon leaped to her feet. Kate half expected her to jump on the table as well, like a cartoon woman who'd just seen a mouse.

"Get him out of here," her father yelled.

Kate looked at him. "Who?"

"The cat."

Mrs. Gordon let out a violent sneeze, followed by a whole stream of sneezes. She grabbed a handful of tissues and blew holes in all of them. Eyes bigger than saucers, she held up her hands as if shielding herself from something she didn't want to see. Then she turned and fled into the kitchen, slamming the door so hard that its hinges rattled.

Kate didn't dare look at her dad.

He made a noise in his throat, and it sounded suspiciously like laughter. To cover her own smile, Kate scooped up young Persy and hugged him so tightly that he yowled. The Gorgon wasn't just allergic to cats, she was terrified of them, the same way Kate was terrified of spiders. Dad teased her about it all the time.

Would he tease Mrs. Gordon as well?

10

"GIANT CATS WITH BIG TEETH," Holly said, baring her own. "That's what we need. Just like those giant spiders in Harry Potter."

Kate shuddered.

"Leopards and tigers," Holly went on, "hordes of them."

"And a lion tamer," Kate said.

After shutting Persy in Kate's bedroom, Dad had driven her back to Holly's house. Mrs. Gordon had taken off in her own car, still sneezing like crazy. Before she left, Kate had apologized to the Gorgon because her father insisted.

"I'm not *really* scared of cats," Mrs. Gordon had said, leaning on the kitchen table for support. "It's just that I'm terribly allergic."

Kate didn't let on, but she understood exactly how it felt to be scared witless of something that other people didn't even flinch at. But Mrs. Gordon had it far worse than Kate did. Cats and kittens were all over the place. So were spiders, but mostly they hung out where you couldn't see them. They weren't likely to show up in kids' doll carriages or washing their paws on a velvet cushion.

"Was your dad freaked out?" Holly said. "Like was he mad at you, or anything?"

Kate shrugged. "I don't think so."

With Dad it was hard to tell. He rarely got worked up over people, just over moths and butterflies. Tomorrow was his first cooking lesson with Liz. Maybe he'd learn to get worked up over her instead. That's what Kate wanted. So did Holly. They wanted it so badly, they could almost taste it—like Holly's favorite buttercrunch ice cream and the sausage pizza from Alfie's that Kate couldn't ever get enough of.

Holly switched off the bedroom light.

Her ceiling glowed in the dark. Amid the herds of wild horses galloping across it were stars and planets that Liz had stuck up to keep Holly entertained when she couldn't walk and was confined to her bed.

Kate picked out the constellation for Pegasus—or pretended she did. The night sky was still a big mystery to her, but if she squinted hard enough and turned her head a certain way, well, maybe that really was a magic horse with wings up there.

* * *

There were days, Holly decided, when it was wicked cool to have your mom for a riding instructor. Other days, it wasn't so hot, like right now.

"Holly, use your *legs*," Mom hollered. "Drive Magician forward. Engage his rear end."

"Hands lower," she yelled at Kristina. "You are *not* a saddle seat rider." Then turning fast, she rounded on Sue who was posting on the wrong diagonal. "I'll pretend I didn't see that."

Even Jennifer didn't escape.

Mom waved her into the middle of the arena and gave her a mini-lecture about the correct aids for an extended trot. "It doesn't mean go faster; it means you lengthen the horse's stride."

The only one not getting the sharp edge of Mom's tongue was Angela. Somehow, in the past week, she'd come to grips with her new horse. Mom hadn't said a word about Mrs. Dean except that she'd insisted on private lessons for Angela, and Mom had provided them by working extra hours to fit everything in. This was the first time Angela and Ragtime had appeared together in public, and much as Holly hated to admit it, they made an impressive team.

Nose almost vertical, Ragtime floated across the arena with hooves that seemed to barely touch the ground. Angela sat tall and straight in the saddle. For once her arms and legs weren't all over the place. You couldn't tell if she was giving Ragtime subtle aids or if he was doing this all by himself.

Holly shot a glance at Kate.

She was in the observation room, leaning forward, nose almost pressed against the glass, and Holly knew exactly what was going through Kate's mind—the same thing that was going through hers. Angela and Ragtime would definitely qualify for the Festival of Horses, and once there, they'd be almost impossible to beat.

* * *

The photo Kate had been dreading finally turned up on the barn's Facebook page. Angela had taken it at the December show when Kate and Brad had been sitting together at lunch. Innocently, the caption read: *Having fun with friends at Fox Meadow Hunt Club.*

There were other photos, but this one stood out like a sore thumb among the shots of Angela and Skywalker soaring over jumps that her mother had taken. There were none of Angela's disastrous dressage test, which was hardly surprising. It had dragged her score so low that she'd failed to qualify.

"Big deal," Holly said. "Nathan won't see it."

"Are you sure?" Kate said.

Nathan's Facebook fan page was managed by a team of publicists at the studio, and he rarely bothered with his personal page. He hadn't posted anything new since Thanksgiving, and that was a shot of the caves they were shooting in. They looked dark and creepy—perfect for the *Moonlight* film, Holly proclaimed.

She pinned Kate with a look. "You've got to tell him about Brad."

Kate shrugged. "There's nothing to tell."

They'd been arguing about this for weeks and getting nowhere. Holly kept needling her for details, but Kate didn't have any. The most exciting thing Brad had done was squeeze her hand too hard when she fell over on the ski trail, plus he'd adjusted her knee brace at the pool, but that was—

Holly's e-mail pinged. "Oh, fun!"

"What?" Kate said.

"The barn's winter party. It's a blast. Last year we had a Spanish Fiesta."

Kate scanned Mrs. Dean's message: All riding team members, their families, and friends were invited to the club for a Hawaiian luau. It promised live entertainment, hula lessons, real leis, and an authentic buffet complete with mahi-mahi.

"What's that?" Holly said.

"Dolphin."

Holly screamed. "You can't eat Flipper."

"Chill out," Kate said. "It's a totally different animal. It's a *dolphinfish*." She skimmed the invitation again. "I guess we're supposed to dress up." Mrs. Dean was famous for throwing costume parties. At the Labor Day party, Kate had gone as the headless horseman. It was so hot inside her voluminous cloak that she'd almost melted.

Holly put a hand to her head. "But I've got *nothing* to wear," she said. "Magician ate my grass skirt."

"And mine's at the dry cleaners," Kate said. She gave Holly a wicked look. "Can you imagine Mrs. Dean in a lei and grass skirt?"

"Dancing the hula?"

"With bare feet?" Kate said, shuddering. Mrs. Dean was thinner than a stick insect and about as cuddly.

Bending over her laptop, Holly forwarded the e-mail to Adam and Brad, then sent it to Nathan as well.

"Nuh-uh," Kate said. "He's in New Zealand, re-member? He's not gonna fly home for one of Mrs. Dean's parties."

Or would he?

He'd shown up unexpectedly at the last one. Holly and Adam had known he'd be there, but Kate hadn't. This was before she'd met Brad. Okay, so what if Nathan *did* show up and Brad was—?

No, that was stupid.

Nathan was on a movie location in the mountains of New Zealand, miles from civilization and living in a tent. Granted, it was a pretty luxurious tent with electricity, real beds, and hot water. But its cell service was awful.

Kate hadn't heard from Nathan in over a week. She had no idea if he'd gotten her text message or if he was ignoring her. That was Holly's take on it, anyway. She said that Nathan was mad because Brad Piretti had answered Kate's cell phone and that Nathan was giving her the cold shoulder.

But Kate refused to believe it.

Nathan's phone wasn't working; that's all it was. Grabbing her canes, Kate hauled herself off Holly's spare bed and put weight on both legs.

Her knee held with only a mild twinge.

It really was improving. Tomorrow she would ask the physical therapist if she could at least sit on a horse. With help and a mounting block, Kate was sure she'd be able to climb onto Plug or even Daisy.

Holly's e-mail pinged again, this time with a message from Liz.

TO: The Timber Ridge Riding Team
SUBJECT: Dressage Clinic
Mrs. Dean has kindly arranged for Lockie Malone to conduct a dressage clinic on Saturday, January 24, at 10 o'clock. All team members are encouraged to attend.

"Lockie Malone?" Holly said. "Who's that?"

"The guy who found Ragtime for Angela, remember?" Kate said. She'd forgotten to tell Holly about the photo she'd seen in *Young Rider*. "He rode as a junior at the National five years ago, won a medal, and then kind of disappeared."

"That's it!" Holly said. "Let's give The Gorgon a medal and—"

"—she'll disappear, too," Kate finished.

Holly burst out laughing. So did Kate. She loved it when she and Holly had exactly the same thoughts, even if they were totally off the wall.

* * *

Kate stepped up her exercise program. The qualifying show was three weeks away; the weekend before it was Mrs. Dean's party and the dressage clinic. Kate didn't give a rap about the party, but she was determined to be fit enough to attend the clinic, preferably on her own horse. If not, she could sit on the sidelines and still learn a lot from a rider like Lockie Malone. According to Angela he was brilliant.

"You've never met him," Jennifer said. "So how do you know?"

"I just do," Angela snapped.

Ragtime gave her a nudge. She ignored him, the way she'd always ignored Skywalker. Kate wanted to smack her. Angela had a magnificent horse dying to be loved, and all she cared about were the blue ribbons and trophies he'd help her to win.

"Bratface," Holly muttered.

Three days later, Kate rode the chairlift with Brad to watch his sister beat Angela in the giant slalom. The next afternoon, they cheered Jennifer to victory against Angela in the club's junior tennis tournament.

Mrs. Dean complained, *loudly.*

Waving her stopwatch and score sheets, she ripped into the judges and insisted they'd made a mistake. But they finally overruled her, and Angela didn't get the gold medals her mother coveted.

But Angela shrugged it off, or pretended to. While Mrs. Dean was making a fool of herself, Angela hung out with Courtney and Kristina, sipping soft drinks and comparing their French manicures. Angela wore a new perfume. She said it had been created especially for her.

* * *

Holly swung into high gear over Mrs. Dean's party. Shawls and camisoles tumbled out of drawers as she ransacked her room for the perfect outfits. Necklaces and earrings spilled from jewelry boxes; silk flowers appeared like magic. A purple tie-dye sarong landed on Kate's bed.

She eyed it suspiciously. "What's this?"

"Wrap it around you," Holly said, bouncing across the room. From her closet, she pulled another sarong and knotted it around her slender waist. Its turquoise fringe brushed against her bare legs. "Like this."

"Why can't I wear shorts?" Kate said.

Ignoring her, Holly rummaged through a box and produced two tankini tops. She handed Kate a purple one with white flowers on it that matched her sarong. "Wear this as well."

"Okay." Grumpily, Kate pulled it on.

"Not over your sweatshirt, stupid."

"But it's *cold*," Kate said, faking a shiver.

"It won't be at the pool," Holly said. "This is a tropical party, a luau. Mrs. Dean will have the heat turned up to a hundred. We'll all be wilting."

Brad had told Kate that he and Adam would be wearing flip-flops and Hawaiian shirts. Holly said they were already bragging about whose was the loudest. Trying not to be obvious, Kate checked her phone in case Nathan had left a message.

Nothing. Not a peep from New Zealand.

11

On Saturday morning, Lockie Malone showed up at the barn in Mrs. Dean's silver Mercedes. Angela said he'd arrived earlier via a private plane that landed at Rutland's municipal airport.

She emphasized the word *municipal* as if it were hugely important, like Kennedy or Logan. If you didn't know better, you'd think he'd just flown in on Air Force One.

Given the hoopla, Kate expected Lockie Malone to be stuck up and distant, but he wasn't. Mrs. Dean's latest fix-all for Angela strolled down the aisle, greeting each horse and rider with a genuine smile that said he knew exactly where they were coming from. He'd already been there and done that and was now sharing it with others.

Kate warmed to him at once.

Even though she'd decided not to risk riding, she'd be with Lockie in the center of the arena, soaking up every word he said. So would Liz, although Kate wasn't too sure how Liz felt about him. Hands clasped behind her back, she stood to one side as Mrs. Dean and Angela fawned over Lockie Malone as if he were their protégé.

"You *must* come to our little party tonight," Mrs. Dean said, laying a hand on Lockie's arm. Her crimson nails stood out like drops of blood against his brown leather jacket.

Gracefully, Lockie Malone moved out of reach. "Thank you," he said, "but I'll be leaving right after the clinic."

"Nooo," Angela wailed. "You can't."

From behind a wave of black hair, she looked up at Lockie and batted her eyelashes. Kate half expected her to coo like a dove. Angela's white breeches were spotless, her boots shone, and there wasn't even a smudge of dirt on her Irish sweater or her designer vest which probably cost more than Kate's saddle. It was obvious Angela hadn't bothered to groom her new horse and wasn't about to tack him up either. Kristina was already doing it for her.

"I'm afraid I must," Lockie replied. "The pilot will be waiting."

As if pilots and airplanes were of no consequence,

Mrs. Dean gave a loud sniff, then wobbled off on her high heels toward the arena's observation room. She had her own special chair with armrests and a soft cushion that she kept covered with a dust sheet. Nobody else was allowed to use it.

"What's that stink?" Holly whispered.

Kate sniffed. "Angela's perfume?"

"Smells like paint stripper," Holly said, wrinkling her nose. She ducked into Magician's stall and finished tacking him up.

One by one, horses and riders headed for the indoor arena. Lockie Malone hung back and fell into step beside Kate. She was walking slowly, still using a cane. It was easy to trip in the barn.

"What happened?" he said.

"I fell."

"Off a horse?"

"Skiing," Kate said.

"Too bad," he said. "How long before you can ride again?"

Kate hesitated. "I'm going to a show next weekend."

"That's not answering my question," Lockie said. There was a hint of laughter in his voice. "Are you planning to ride in it?"

"Yes," Kate blurted. "But—"

"The doctor said no?" Lockie said, putting a hand

under Kate's elbow to steady her. "Or your parents did?"

"It's just my dad," Kate said. "And Liz. She's worried I'll make it worse."

"And what about you?" Lockie said. "What do you think?"

"I want to ride."

"Why?"

"It's the last qualifying show," Kate said. "If I don't ride, I won't have a chance at the Festival of Horses in April." They'd reached the arena's double doors. Inside, the riding team circled their horses, warming up. Lockie seemed in no hurry to get to them.

Gently, he said, "There are times when it's all about taking chances. You took a chance by skiing, and you'll take another by riding in the show." There was a pause. "Are you ready to accept the consequences of your decision if it doesn't work out?"

Kate swallowed hard.

"Think about it," Lockie said. "And—"

Mrs. Dean tapped on the observation room's glass window. "Hurry up," she said. "The girls are waiting."

* * *

Lockie Malone took the Timber Ridge team back to basics—a flat-footed walk, a working trot, and a relaxed

117

canter that didn't come anywhere near collection. It was clear to Kate that he wanted to see where everyone was coming from.

Almost immediately, Ragtime acted up.

He'd been snorting and tossing his head ever since Angela got on his back. Ears pinned, he was now two steps away from turning himself inside out. This was really weird. He'd been such a bulletproof horse. Even Lockie, who'd found him for Mrs. Dean, looked puzzled.

"Come here," he said to Angela.

She trotted over.

Lockie examined her bridle. He checked Ragtime's bit and made sure his girth wasn't pinching. "Get off," he said.

Angela stared at him. "Why?"

"Please, don't argue."

With a look that would stop a stampede, Angela swung her leg over Ragtime's neck and slid to the ground. In one fluid movement, Lockie vaulted onto Ragtime's back. The horse shuddered for a moment and then stood still. Lockie gathered up his reins and moved away. He took Ragtime onto the rail. No sign of head tossing or bad behavior. It was like a totally different horse.

Everyone stopped to watch . . . except Angela. She

folded her arms and acted like she didn't care as Lockie rode a small circle and then back to her. Up went Ragtime's handsome head, and the whites of his eyes showed. Again Lockie pulled away, and the horse settled down. They trotted across the diagonal.

Ragtime gave a playful buck.

"Yee, haw!" Jennifer yelled. "Ride 'em, cowboy."

Lockie grinned, then pushed Ragtime into a flawless fourth-level test—voltes, half passes, pirouettes at the canter, and an extended trot that left Kate gasping for more. This horse could do it all, and then some. But when Ragtime got anywhere near Angela, he spazzed out. Lockie's eyes had begun to water.

"It's your perfume," he told Angela.

She stamped her foot. "No way."

"Go and wash off," he said, pointing toward the barn. "Whatever you're wearing is driving your horse nuts."

* * *

An hour after Lockie left with Mrs. Dean, the girls switched from discussing his clinic to that night's party. Angela had disappeared, angry over being singled out. She'd slammed Ragtime into his stall and hadn't even bothered to take his saddle off.

Kate did it for her.

She rubbed Ragtime down and put his blanket on. Across the aisle, Holly brushed Magician with vigorous strokes. In the next stall, Jennifer groomed Rebel until he shone like a newly minted penny. Kristina had Cody on the crossties, picking out his feet. Sue and Robin hugged their horses and fed them carrots.

Tapestry gave a soft whicker.

Kate limped into her stall. She wrapped her arms around Tapestry's neck and wished that Lockie had seen her in action. On his way out he'd said she looked like a nice horse, but—

"What's a *muu-muu?*" Jennifer said.

"A Hawaiian tent dress," Holly said. "With lots of flowers on it."

"Who'd wanna wear *that?*" Sue said.

Holly grinned. "Mrs. Dean?"

Then Robin and Kristina chimed in, and their voices got lost in a flurry of excitement over what they'd be wearing to Mrs. Dean's party. Kate had agreed to go, but she wasn't looking forward to it. She'd much rather talk about Lockie Malone's dressage clinic.

* * *

Holly insisted on another makeover. "You can't go to the party like this," she said. "Your hair's a mess and you've got a zit."

"Two," Kate said. They'd erupted on her chin that morning. They always did whenever she was nervous or excited about something like Lockie Malone's clinic.

Holly got busy with foundation and concealer. This time she let Kate watch. When Holly had given Kate a makeover for the Labor Day party, she'd covered the mirror with a towel and Kate wasn't allowed to see the results until Holly was all finished. Kate had barely recognized herself.

Expertly, Holly dusted Kate's cheeks with blush, smeared glittery mauve shadow on her eyelids, and brushed her lashes with three coats of iridescent mascara the color of Tapestry's new winter blanket. Kate gave a little shudder. It looked as if she'd just collided with a pair of giant blue spiders.

"We're all doing this," Holly said. "Lots and lots of make-up. It'll drive Angela wild." She brandished a hot pink lipstick.

Kate put up her hands. "No."

"Smile," Holly said, and before Kate could object, her lips were painted the same shade as Courtney's latest tennis dress. Then Holly tucked a matching hibiscus behind Kate's ear.

"It's way over the top," Kate grumbled.

"It's supposed to be," Holly said. "It's a disguise. You can pretend to be someone else for the evening."

"Why?"

"Duh-uh," Holly said. "To have fun."

As Kate tried to knot her sarong the way Holly did, she thought about her best friend's words. Much as she hated to admit it, they were totally on target.

Kate *had* enjoyed hiding behind her witch's costume at Halloween. She'd loved wearing the glamorous dress she'd bought at a thrift shop for Holly's birthday party and the magical one she'd worn in the *Moonlight* scene. For a few precious hours they'd allowed her to be someone else entirely instead of awkward old Kate who always wore muck boots and didn't know how to tie a sarong or talk to cute boys.

* * *

Kate's father came to pick them up. To her utter amazement, he was wearing a red-and-yellow Hawaiian shirt that matched Liz's long dress.

"Did you guys collaborate?" Holly said.

He winked at her. "We'll never tell."

Holly climbed into the back seat with Kate. "It's working," she whispered.

"What is?"

"The cooking lessons, you dummy."

Kate had forgotten all about them. She'd been so focused on her knee and the show and Lockie's clinic that everything else had flown out the window. She stole a glance at Liz, sitting beside Dad in the front seat. Holly had given her a makeover, too. Liz's eyes sparkled, her cheeks glowed, and Kate hoped it wasn't just because of Holly's skill with cosmetics. Liz even had a flower in *her* hair. Kate hadn't yet told her that she planned to ride in the show. Maybe later tonight would be a good time.

* * *

The party was in full swing by the time they got there. Lights flashed, the disco ball blinked, and rock music thumped from all the speakers. Girls wearing leis and grass skirts flirted with boys in Hawaiian print shirts. A couple of them doing back-flips into the pool and spectacular cannonballs that soaked everyone within ten feet.

Angela squealed. She wore a white bikini and enough flowers in her hair to decorate a float at Mardi Gras. Her perfume overwhelmed the pool's chlorine.

"Good thing Ragtime's not here," Holly said.

A cute-looking guy with streaky blond hair and shoulders like a weight lifter leaned against the wall. Angela kept shooting glances at him.

"Who's that?" Kate said.

"Channing Alexander," Holly said. "He's the son of

one of Mrs. Dean's old school friends. She always trots him out at parties like this. It's someone for Angela to drool over."

"Does he like her?"

Holly shrugged. "Who knows?"

But it was clear that Angela liked him. She followed him around like a big-eyed puppy, hanging on his every word. At the buffet table, she filled his plate with chicken wings and pineapple chunks, not even giving him a chance to choose for himself.

"Is that the dolphin?" Holly said, eyeing a platter of grilled fish.

"Mahi-mahi," said Kate's father.

Liz helped herself to a generous serving. "I love this stuff."

"You do?" Holly said. "Since when?"

"My honeymoon in Hawaii."

Her lips trembled. For a few seconds Kate thought Liz would bust into tears, but Dad saved the day.

"There are some amazing butterflies in Hawaii," he said, leading Holly's mom to an empty table. "Let me tell you about the Chinese Swallowtail my team found."

"Phew," Holly said. "I thought Mom was about to lose it there." She set down her plate. "I'm not hungry. Let's find the guys and go for a swim."

"Sure," Kate said.

They headed for the pool. Brad and Adam were already there, hanging out at a bistro table with Jennifer and Sue. All of a sudden, there was a scream and a splash.

"*Help!*"

12

WITHOUT STRIPPING OFF HER SARONG, Kate dived in. She surfaced beside Angela. Her arms thrashed; she waved and yelled again. Was she drowning or trying to get someone's attention? Kate reached for Angela's shoulders.

A life-saving ring landed beside them.

"Go away," Angela snarled, spitting water. "You've ruined everything." She spun around and swam toward the edge where Channing Alexander was still busy showing off his muscles to Courtney and Kristina James. He didn't seem to realize that Angela had gone missing.

Holly helped Kate out of the pool.

"I feel like an idiot," Kate said.

"Don't," Holly replied. "Angela's the idiot, not you."

"So is that guy," Kate said. "Channing what's-his-name."

He hadn't even bothered to give Angela his towel. She stood beside him, shivering, with bedraggled blossoms falling from her hair like dead flowers while he boasted how fast he could swim the freestyle. "I bet I could beat Michael Phelps."

Holly shed her sarong. Beneath it she wore a turquoise tankini. "I'll fix him," she said to Kate, then sidled up to Channing Alexander. "Wanna race?"

"With you?" he said, laughing.

"Yes," she said. "You pick the stroke."

"Butterfly," he said. "Four lengths."

"Six." Holly headed for the deep end of the pool and positioned herself for a racing dive. "Eat my wake," she said, as he swaggered up beside her.

Someone yelled, "*Go!*"

At the first turn, Holly was ahead. People abandoned the buffet table and stood around the pool. All eyes were on Kate's best friend as she churned through the water like a dolphin. Poor Channing Alexander didn't stand a chance. Holly beat him by almost two lengths.

* * *

"Your makeup's a mess," Kate said. They were in the ladies' room, drying off. She wrung water from her sarong over the sink.

"So's yours," Holly replied, toweling her hair.

Kate looked in the mirror and groaned. "I guess it wasn't waterproof, huh?" Mascara trickled down her cheeks like iridescent blue tears; blobs of pink lipstick had migrated onto her chin. There was no sign of the silk flower that Holly had stuck behind her ear.

"Are you gonna talk to Mom?" Holly said.

"About the show?"

"Yes."

"Think this is a good time?" Kate said, casting about for an excuse to put it off. She was dreading Liz's reaction, to say nothing of her father's. She flexed her knee. This was the first time she'd gone without her brace.

Holly nodded. "Everyone's in a good mood."

They found a bottle of body lotion and used it to clean off their make-up. Kate felt much better without it. She retied her damp sarong and followed Holly back to the party. Their parents were doing a slow dance. For a moment or two, Kate forgot all about the horse show and her knee and just enjoyed watching them.

"Sweet," Holly said.

Kate smiled. "Yeah."

Dad and Liz made a really cute couple, even if their matching outfits were kind of cheesy. When the music ended, they returned to the table, and just as Kate was about to launch into her well-rehearsed speech, Liz interrupted.

"Change of plans for next weekend."

"Oh?" Holly said. "Like what?" She gave Kate a sharp nudge as if to say, *Keep quiet and listen.*

Her mother shot a quick glance at Kate's dad. "Ben's invited me to an art show in Boston."

"And a butterfly exhibit," he said.

"We'll be staying over, too," Liz went on. "Will you girls be okay on your own for a couple of nights, or should I ask Aunt Bea to come and stay?"

"What about Angela?" Holly blurted.

Liz gave a little sigh. "Mrs. Dean has already arranged for a trainer from Larchwood to come and get Ragtime on Friday afternoon. Angela will be under his care at the show."

It took a few minutes for this to sink in. Without Liz, Kate had no way of getting to the show, assuming Liz had agreed she was fit enough to compete in the first place. Miserably, she got up and left the table.

Brad ambled toward her. "Wanna dance?"

"I guess." Kate shrugged.

"Is your knee okay?" he said. "I mean—?"

"Yeah, it's fine," Kate said.

But it really didn't matter any more. Without the horse show to work toward, she wouldn't care if her stupid knee decided to fall off.

Clunk!

Onto the ground, like a rusty old hubcap. Despite herself, Kate smiled.

"What's funny?" Brad said.

So Kate told him.

* * *

"There is *one* good thing about all this," Holly said. She and Kate were in the hot tub with Brad and Adam. Most of the other guests had left, and already a couple of bus boys were cleaning off tables and sweeping the floor.

"Oh, yeah?" Kate said. "Like what?"

The swirling water helped to soothe her knee. It had begun to ache again, totally in sync with her rotten mood.

"Like *my* mom and *your* dad? They're going *away* for the weekend?" Holly said, shifting closer to Adam.

Kate hadn't even thought of that.

"If Mrs. Dean hadn't gone behind Mom's back and hired another trainer," Holly went on, "Mom would've been taking Angela to the show, and your dad would have gone to Boston by himself, or he'd have taken The Gorgon instead."

"I guess you're right," Kate said, shuddering.

Adam said, "I've got an idea."

"Ding, ding," Holly said. "News at eleven."

"Brat," Adam said and shoved her off the seat. She

stuck out her tongue and disappeared beneath the surface in a flurry of warm bubbles.

"C'mon, dude," Brad said. "What's up?"

"How about I kind of *borrow* my mom's truck and come to get Magician so Kate can ride in the show?" he said, as Holly surfaced.

"Nuh-uh," she said, spurting water at him. "You're not licensed to pull a horse trailer."

Adam's face fell. "Oh, right."

"But I am," Brad said.

Holly's eyes lit up. "Seriously?"

"Yeah, seriously. It's the same license I use to drive Dad's heavy equipment."

"Awesome," Holly said.

She rattled off a list of chores—get help at the barn for Saturday, find out if her mom had scratched Kate from the show, and, above all, keep it a secret! Kate's head began to spin. This wasn't right. She couldn't just up and go to a horse show without telling Liz and her dad about it.

Could she?

* * *

On Sunday, Holly hit the show's web site and checked the list of competitors. Kate's name was still there. Great, Mom hadn't gotten around to canceling her. With luck, she'd forget. But they wouldn't know for sure until they got to Larchwood Equestrian Center first thing Saturday morning.

For the next three days, Holly schooled Magician while Kate doubled up her exercises at the club. By Wednesday evening, Kate said she felt confident enough to ride.

They had the barn to themselves.

Mom was at her cooking lesson with Ben, and Angela and Kristina were nowhere to be seen. Sue and Robin had offered to handle barn chores on Saturday and Jennifer would come to the show with them. It was all falling into place, except that Brad refused to pull the barn's trailer.

"Not without permission," he said, giving Kate a leg-up onto Magician. He was so strong that he almost tossed her over the other side. "I'd lose my license if a cop stopped us."

"Okay, genius," Holly said. "Now what?"

"I'll borrow Mr. Evans's trailer," Brad said.

Holly knew all the horse owners in Winfield, but she'd never heard of this one. "Who is he?"

"A farmer," Brad said. "He cuts hay from our ski slopes every summer for his cows."

"Is his trailer a cattle truck?"

Brad shrugged. "Dunno."

"Then we'd better check," Holly said. Cattle trucks had no partitions and no rubber mats on the floors. Horses could slip and fall. They'd already had one mishap with Magician at this competition; they didn't need another one, especially when Mom wasn't around.

* * *

At the far end of the arena, Kate worked at getting Magician to bend around her bad leg. It was beginning to throb. What was it Lockie Malone had said? *A good rider gets a lot out of a horse without taking a lot out of him.*

Kate eased off with the pressure. Her leg felt instantly better, and Magician curved into a perfect twenty-meter circle. That was something else Lockie emphasized. *Not nineteen meters, not twenty-one meters, but twenty meters—exactly.* After that, he'd talked about corners and diagonals and how those could make or break a first-level test.

Her cell phone rang.

Kate almost ignored it because she was about to start jumping, but it stopped, then rang again almost immediately.

Uh-oh. This had to be important.

She slowed Magician to a walk, pulled out her phone, and answered it without bothering to check caller ID.

"Hi," Nathan said. "Are you okay?"

"Yes, no," Kate said, flustered. She dropped her reins. Magician ambled toward Holly and Brad. Not a good idea. Quickly, she pulled him in the other direction.

"What's wrong?" Nathan said.

Kate hadn't told him about her skiing accident or bum knee. She would have if he'd gotten back to her after that last text message she sent from the pool when Brad answered Nathan's call.

Keeping her head averted, Kate gave him a quick rundown but left out the part about going to the show without Liz's permission. Holly and Brad were setting up jumps and didn't appear to have noticed she was letting Magician plod along like a sleepy old cart horse.

"I've sent you tickets," Nathan said, after commiserating with her about the accident. "For the *Moonlight* premiere."

"When is it?"

"Second weekend in April," he said. "School break."

It sounded good to Kate. The Festival of Horses was a week later—assuming she'd even make it that far.

"Where's the show?" Nathan said.

"Larchwood."

"That's where Adam rides, right?"

The connection was so weak that Kate had to cover her other ear so she could hear him. It didn't help that Holly was yelling at her.

"Hustle, Kate. We're waiting."

"I've gotta go," Kate said. "I'll text you later."

"Okay, bye," Nathan said, and he hung up.

Feeling somehow deflated, Kate pulled herself together and concentrated on Magician. She trotted him over the cavalettis, then faced him at the brush jump. Ears pricked, he snorted and skittered sideways as if to say, *Finally, we're gonna do something fun!*

* * *

After Kate finished schooling Magician, Brad drove her and Holly to Mr. Evans's farm to check out his trailer. A stocky chestnut gelding whickered the moment they entered the barn. He had a stumpy tail, mismatched eyes, and an enormous blaze that covered his entire nose.

"Pardner!" Kate shrieked.

Behind her, someone chuckled. "And if I'm remembering right, you're the young lady I met at Rowley's auction. Did you ever find yourself the perfect horse?"

Kate turned. A ten-gallon hat shaded most of the

man's blotchy red birthmark, but it didn't hide his welcoming smile. He held out his hand. "Earl Evans."

"Hi," she said. "I like your horse."

She hadn't liked him at the auction. Among the Thoroughbreds and Arabians for sale, Pardner stood out like a truck in a parking lot full of sports cars. Everyone had laughed at him, including her. She felt herself blush.

"Ayup, he's a keeper," said Mr. Evans.

As he stroked Pardner's homely face, Kate wondered how they'd be able to ask if Mr. Evans's trailer was suitable for horses without sounding rude.

"About your trailer," Brad said. "Could we—?"

"Follow me," said Mr. Evans.

He led them outside. Beneath the barn's floodlight stood a gleaming navy blue trailer. Its back ramp was down. The white interior shone; the thick rubber mats were brand new. A padded partition bar ran down the centerline.

"Let's make sure the hitch works with your truck," Mr. Evans said.

Brad jumped into his cab and backed up to the trailer. Mr. Evans connected the hitch, plugged in the running lights, and gave Brad a thumbs-up. "Which one of you ladies is riding this weekend?"

"Me," Kate said.

"On your new horse?"

"Mine," Holly said. She explained what had happened at the previous show with Magician getting hurt and how she'd ridden Tapestry instead. "We've sort of swapped horses for a bit."

"Well, good luck to you both," he said.

Brad arranged to pick up the trailer at six o'clock on Saturday morning. That would give them plenty of time to load Magician and be at Larchwood by eight. The show started at nine. Kate's anxiety level jumped another notch. She hated going behind Liz's back like this.

13

WHEN THEY GOT BACK TO HOLLY'S HOUSE, Liz showed off her new cooking skills. She whipped up an omelet with tomatoes, onions, and red peppers, then sprinkled grated cheese on top and added a sprig of fresh parsley.

"Mom, this is awesome," Holly said.

Kate asked for seconds. "Can my father do this?"

"Yes," Liz said. "His omelet had portobello mushrooms, cilantro, and Spanish anchovies."

"Ugh," Kate said.

Liz grinned and sat down, then casually dropped another bombshell. "Aunt Bea's coming for the weekend. She'll be here on Friday at noon. Ben and I are leaving for Boston around five. We'll be back on Sunday evening. Is that okay with you girls?"

"Mom!" Holly wailed. "*We're not babies.*"

"I know," Liz said. "It was Aunt Bea's idea. She called to see about coming down for Kate's show. When I told her Kate wasn't competing and that I was going away with Ben, she said she was coming anyway."

Swallowing hard, Kate looked at Holly.

They were totally cooked. They might be able to pull the wool over Liz's eyes, but they'd never be able to pull it over Aunt Bea's.

* * *

"Okay," Holly said. "Time for Plan B."

"Which is?" Kate said.

Holly pulled a face. "That's the trouble," she said. "I don't *know*."

They'd washed the dishes, raved about Liz's omelet, and escaped to Holly's bedroom. But no matter how they sliced and diced the situation, they couldn't see a way around it. Aunt Bea would be onto them like hounds on a fox.

"We've got to tell her," Kate said.

"She'll forbid you."

"Probably," Kate said. "But what else can we do?"

A gleam entered Holly's eyes. This usually meant trouble of one sort or another. Kate put up a warning hand.

"No, wait," Holly said. "I think I've got it. We'll

have Brad truck Magician to Larchwood on Friday night. Adam will fix it so that he's got a stall. Then on Saturday morning, we'll tell Aunt Bea we want to go and watch the show because Angela's competing."

"Yeah, right," Kate said. "She'll believe that like she'll believe cats can fly. Besides, how would we get there?"

"Brad will take us," Holly said, "or Adam will. Then you can jump on Magician and win the class."

"It's not about winning," Kate said. "It's about qualifying, remember?"

"Pfftt," Holly said. "Details."

Magazines fell off her bed as she flipped onto her back and stared at the ceiling. Kate could almost hear the wheels turning inside Holly's head. "Okay, here's what we'll do," she said.

Kate knew better than to interrupt.

"I'm going to e-mail her," Holly said. "I'll swear Aunt Bea to secrecy and then I'll tell her what's going on—all of it."

"Why?"

"Because Aunt Bea's a mystery writer. She loves to solve problems, and we've got a big one."

* * *

Kate counted the hours. She exercised at the club and schooled Magician till they were both covered in sweat.

Her knee held up. She rode without the brace because you couldn't get good leg contact with a lump of rigid plastic between you and your horse. They jumped the double oxer, the parallel bars, and the wall. So far, so good.

Holly yelled from the doorway. "Aunt Bea's here."

It was late on Friday afternoon. Liz and Ben had already left for Boston. The Larchwood trainer had loaded Ragtime onto his red-and-black trailer and taken off. There was no sign of Angela or Mrs. Dean.

Kate halted Magician. "Where?"

"In Mom's office," Holly said.

They hadn't gotten any real feedback from Aunt Bea about their problem, just a vague comment that they needed to *talk about it*—grown-up speak for "Are you kidding me?"

"Give me fifteen," Kate said.

She cooled Magician off, rubbed him down, and joined Holly in her mother's cramped office. Aunt Bea sat in Liz's swivel chair, knitting furiously. Rainbow-colored yarn spilled from her lap.

Without dropping a stitch, Aunt Bea nailed the problem. "You've got a plot," she said, jabbing the air with her needles. "And you want me to be a part of it, right?"

Holly nodded. "Yes."

"Kate, show me your knee," Aunt Bea said.

Kate pulled off her boot and rolled up her breeches. The bruise had faded to pale mauve and an icky shade of yellow. It wasn't nearly as colorful as Aunt Bea's socks.

"Does it hurt?" she said.

"No." Kate hesitated. "Well, only a little bit."

Aunt Bea set down her knitting. "Okay, here's the deal. If Kate's doc gives her the go-ahead to compete, then I'm on board."

"It's late," Holly said, looking at her watch. "Doctors have gone home."

"Try anyway," Aunt Bea said.

Kate punched in the ortho-doc's number. She got voice mail. "If this is an emergency, please call—"

"Call your physical therapist," Holly said.

Aunt Bea nodded. "That would do."

She answered on the first ring. "Come and see me, right now," she said, and hung up.

* * *

Thirty minutes later, Kate passed all the tests. She pushed and pulled on command and didn't even wince when the physical therapist twisted her knee like a pretzel.

"Well done," she said. "I didn't think you'd make it."

"Then she's okay to ride?" said Aunt Bea.

"Yes," said the therapist. "And good luck."

"Whoopee!" Holly punched the air with her fist.

Kate collapsed into a chair as if she'd just run a marathon. But inside, she glowed. Despite Holly's belief that they could skate around the rules, it felt really good to have a grown-up behind them. Liz wouldn't be mad at Kate for competing now that she had Aunt Bea's stamp of approval.

As they drove back to the barn, Holly called Brad on her cell phone sounding like mission control at a space launch.

"Ten hours and counting," she said.

Brad would show up with Mr. Evans's trailer at six-thirty the next morning. Sue and Robin would handle barn chores. Jennifer was primed to come with them.

All systems were go.

* * *

It began to snow as they entered the showgrounds, but that didn't matter. Everything would be held inside. The Larchwood arenas were even bigger than the ones at Fox Meadow.

Adam met them in the parking lot.

Holly jumped out of Brad's truck and kissed him. The others tumbled out behind her. It had been a squish, fitting them all into seatbelts. Aunt Bea declared her hips would never be the same again.

"I've got a stall for Magician," Adam said.

This was way better than keeping him in the trailer and slogging through snowdrifts between classes. While Holly and Jennifer gathered up Kate's tack and grooming box, Kate unloaded Magician and followed Adam into Larchwood's luxurious barn.

An ocean of gleaming wood and polished fittings met Kate's eyes. Rakes, shovels, and brooms lined up perfectly on brass hooks. No cobwebs hung from the rafters. Each stall had a shiny red nameplate and a well-groomed horse sticking its head over the door. Even the muck buckets sparkled.

"Just one problem," Adam said.

"What?"

"You're stabled next to Angela."

Ragtime whinnied when he saw Magician. Kate led Holly's gelding into a roomy stall ankle deep in fresh shavings. A black haynet stuffed with Timothy and alfalfa hung from a metal ring; the automatic waterer waited for a thirsty horse to trigger it.

Jennifer said, "I'll get your number."

"Thanks," Kate said and crossed her fingers that Liz hadn't scratched her. She'd never been overwhelmed at a show before, but this one would take a little getting used to. Loudspeakers blared, uniformed grooms brushed horses on the crossties, and riders in earnest conversation with their trainers walked by.

"Hang in there," Aunt Bea said. "Just remember that everyone here puts their pants on one leg at a time, and looks like an idiot when they brush their teeth."

Jennifer returned victorious from the show secretary's booth. She had a schedule, the course map, and, best of all, Kate's number, 315. With a sigh of relief she hadn't been scratched, Kate tied it around her waist.

"I *love* it," Holly cried.

Kate looked at her. "Why?"

"It's your birthday—March fifteenth—and Tapestry's, too."

"How'd you figure that?" Kate said, taking it off and having another look.

"Three fifteen," Holly said. "Third month, fifteenth day." She clapped her hands. "It's bound to be lucky."

* * *

Horses and riders milled around the collecting ring as Kate waited for her turn to jump. She would be third to go. The course was a mix of brightly painted oxers and cross-country fences in the same layout as the previous show except for the Liverpool—a formidable water jump—which was now last.

Magician loved water.

He'd probably want to paddle in it. Or worse, he'd want to lie down and roll in it like he did in the stream at Kate's *Moonlight* audition. Afterward, the director said it was what had clinched the role for Kate. Well, that plus the fact that she'd ridden Magician bareback.

"Keep him going," Holly said. "Use your crop if you need to."

Off went the first rider. Two rails down. Then came the second rider with three refusals at the Liverpool. Red-faced, he rode toward Kate, and she recognized him from the December show. He'd had problems at the Liverpool then, as well. In fact, he'd fallen into it.

"Sorry," she mouthed.

He shrugged. "Thanks."

The steward's whistle blew. Kate gathered up her reins and trotted into the ring. In the stands, she caught sight of Aunt Bea and Jennifer sitting with Brad. Beside him was Mr. Evans. He took off his Stetson and waved it.

This wasn't a "hunter over fences" class. It didn't matter about style or form or looking pretty. What mattered was getting over the jumps without refusing or knocking them down. Kate rode through the starting gate and aimed Magician at the crossrail. Over they went, then the brush.

Tightening her grip, Kate swung a left-hand turn toward the stone wall. It looked like a real one, but Kate knew the stones were fake—it wouldn't hurt if a horse banged into them.

"One, two, three," Kate counted.

Magician gathered himself up, and over they went.

Next came the hogsback. It had three red-and-white rails, the middle one higher than the other two. Magician cleared it with inches to spare. Kate began to relax. Magician was on the top of his form and her knee hadn't bothered her once . . . at least, not yet. She cantered a wide loop around the Liverpool and could almost feel Magician giving it the eye.

Four jumps behind her; another four to go—well, five, if you counted the in-and-out combo as two jumps. Next up were the logs. Like the stone wall, the logs weren't real. They fell apart if a horse touched them.

Kate moved into a half-seat.

Magician flew over the logs and landed square. Ahead was the combination, two jumps close together. But as they approached the first one—a stack of hay bales—Kate could feel Magician falter. At the last show, two horses had stopped dead at this jump and made the crowd laugh by snacking on it.

"This is *not* lunch," Kate yelled.

The audience erupted in laughter. Kate heard Holly

cheering. She'd said pretty much the same thing to Tapestry a month earlier.

Kate tapped Magician with her crop.

Over the hay bales they went, one big stride, then the green-and-white parallel bars. The minute they landed, Kate pulled Magician into a hard right to face the double oxer. No big deal, except for a window box full of plastic flowers. Magician rocked back on his haunches, tucked his front legs, and—

Clang!

"Aahhhh," went the audience.

This was the jump that Tapestry almost flubbed. Kate held her breath. She heard the rail wobble in its cups and waited for the inevitable thud that would land her with four faults.

But the rail held.

One more jump to go. The Liverpool loomed like a beach scene. Two vertical black-and-white rails stood in front of a shallow pool. On either side were tall white towers that resembled lifeguard platforms. As they drew closer, Kate half expected to see a shark's fin in the bright blue water.

Jaws, here we come.

Magician hesitated. Kate dug her heels into his sides. "No swimming."

Ears swiveling like antennae, Holly's horse listened.

With what sounded like a sigh of disappointment, he lifted himself up and catapulted over the water. The arena's loudspeaker crackled into life.

"Our first clear round."

More clear rounds would surely follow, but Kate didn't care. Leaning forward, she flung her arms around Magician's neck and dropped a dozen kisses up and down his braided mane.

Just the way Holly always did.

14

DUST FLEW AS A WOMAN in black breeches and a red hoodie brushed Ragtime with vigorous strokes. So far, Angela hadn't made an appearance. Neither had Kristina, which was kind of odd given that she used to ride at this barn and never missed a chance to flirt with Adam, much to Holly's disgust.

"Kristina's home sick," Jennifer said.

She checked her schedule and announced that Angela would be jumping shortly before lunch. Kate pulled off Magician's tack and began to rub him down. He'd barely worked up a sweat.

"Hey there," Mr. Evans called out.

Hand cupped beneath Aunt Bea's elbow, Mr. Evans shepherded her down the aisle, chatting as if they were old friends. To Kate's surprise, Aunt Bea didn't object.

They looked almost as cute as Dad and Liz had the other night.

Holly raised an eyebrow. "Sweet."

"Don't even think about it," Kate whispered. "No more matchmaking. We've got enough to handle."

"They're doing fine without us."

After congratulating Kate on her clear round, Mr. Evans asked what time she'd be riding again.

"Two-thirty," Jennifer said.

Smoothly, she'd taken over Liz's job of keeping horse and rider on track—a huge relief to Kate because she needed someone to tell her where to go and what to do and when to do it. Her brain had gone into hiding.

"Good," said Mr. Evans, "because I'm taking this fine lady out to lunch. Would you believe it, but she's never eaten a real pork barbecue?"

Off they went. The spurs on Mr. Evans's hand-tooled boots tinkled like wind chimes as he linked arms with Aunt Bea, whose shoulder bag bristled with sharp knitting needles.

"Weapons of mass destruction," Adam said.

"Spurs or needles?" Holly said.

Adam grinned. "Both."

Then he and Brad headed for the Larchwood cafeteria to eat lunch and play video games. They promised to be back in time for Kate's dressage test.

One of Magician's braids had come loose and Kate was about to fix it when another Larchwood groom appeared, this time with Angela's tack. He swept into Ragtime's stall. Moments later, Ragtime emerged. The quartermarks on his polished rump were so precise you could play checkers on them.

Kate finished the braid and buckled Magician's cooler. He didn't need anything warmer because the barn was heated. So were the two big indoor arenas, as well as the smaller one where riders warmed up.

"Let's find Angela," Holly said.

Jennifer snapped open a folding chair and sat down with her iPad. "Go ahead," she said. "I'll stick around."

* * *

They cruised Larchwood's upmarket tack shop, grabbed a free calendar for Liz, and headed for the warm-up arena. Knots of anxious parents stood at the rail while riders got yelled at by trainers. In the far corner, Angela looked as if she were having a tussle with Ragtime. The Larchwood trainer was yelling at her, too.

"Uh-oh," Holly said.

But before they got close enough to hear, Angela screamed. The trainer screamed back, then threw up his hands and stormed off. Tears streaming down her face, Angela blundered toward them. Gobs of foam flew from

Ragtime's mouth and splattered on his chest like miniature marshmallows. His eyes showed white.

"Hold up!" Kate cried.

She grabbed Angela's reins. Ragtime skidded to a halt and for a couple of seconds, Kate thought Angela was going to lash out with her crop. Arm raised, she leaned down and Kate got a whiff of her perfume.

"Get off," Kate said. "Now."

"I don't take orders from *you*," Angela snapped.

Holly glared at her. "You're wearing that stinky stuff again. Your horse hates it. Didn't you learn *anything* last week?"

"I am *not* wearing it," Angela said.

Her horse swiveled like a dervish around Kate. She could hardly hold onto him. Pinning his ears, Ragtime squealed and gave a vicious little buck. Angela managed to stay on, but only just. Awkwardly, she slid to the ground.

"There," she said. "Satisfied now?"

"Take him away," Kate said, handing the reins to Holly.

Almost immediately, Ragtime calmed down. By the time Holly had him at the rail, he was back to normal—ears forward, looking around eagerly at all the activity and nudging her pocket for treats.

"I don't need *your* help," Angela said.

Kate couldn't stop herself. "Yes, you do."

For a few moments, their eyes locked, almost in understanding. Fear and anger had turned Angela's face into a battleground—her trainer had disappeared and her horse wouldn't let her come anywhere near him. If Mrs. Dean found out what was going on, she'd have a major meltdown.

Angela scowled. "Why do you want to help me?"

"Because I like Liz," Kate said, "and I like your horse."

"But not me." Angela gave a bitter laugh.

"That's because you never gave me a chance to," Kate said.

But this wasn't the time to argue barn politics. They had to fix Angela's problem. If they didn't, Mrs. Dean would blame Liz, never mind that she'd gone over Liz's head and hired another trainer for the weekend. Edging closer to Angela, Kate sniffed. Yes, she was definitely wearing perfume. No wonder Ragtime had freaked out.

"I told you," Angela said, backing away. "I'm not wearing any."

Her white breeches were identical to the ones she'd worn at Lockie Malone's clinic. Kate couldn't be sure about the ratcatcher shirt. "Do you have any spare breeches?"

"Yeah, tons," Angela said. "Doesn't everyone?"

"I mean here, at the show."

"No." Angela plucked at the number tied around her waist and turned its neat bow into a knot. She looked up. "Why?"

"Because that's where the perfume is. Your breeches reek of it." Kate thought for a minute. This was nuts . . . her helping Angela out of a mess? Holly would never believe it. "Wait here," she told Angela. "Don't go anywhere near Ragtime."

Angela didn't look as if she wanted to.

Dodging other riders, Kate raced for the rail where Ragtime was insisting that Holly feed him a carrot. He practically had his nose in her pocket.

"So, what's the plan?" she said.

Kate lengthened Ragtime's stirrups. "Warm him up, and I'll fix Angela."

"How?"

"By replacing her breeches."

Holly snorted. "Pity you can't replace *her*." She bent her knee for a leg-up and lowered herself gently into Angela's brand new Passier dressage saddle. "Did you tell her I'm gonna ride Ragtime?"

"Not yet," Kate said, patting Ragtime's well-polished neck. "Be good, okay? No more crazies."

His velvety lips nuzzled Kate's hand. He reminded her of Buccaneer, the movie director's horse she'd ridden last summer. He'd do anything for a peppermint Life

Saver. If the cafeteria's vending machines had any, Kate would grab a pack. Maybe Ragtime would like them, too. She left Holly walking Ragtime along the rail, well away from the other horses, and headed back to Angela.

"You didn't ask permission for Holly to ride my horse," she said, pouting.

Kate ignored her. "Come on, let's go."

"Where?"

"The tack shop. You need new clothes."

* * *

It took Angela twice as long as it should have to find the perfect pair of breeches. She'd taken off her perfume-soaked ones, along with her white ratcatcher, and Kate had stuffed them in a plastic bag. Angela told her to dump it in the trash.

"What about my jacket?" she said, modeling her new clothes before the full-length mirror. Kate caught a glimpse of the price tags and shuddered. The breeches and shirt cost more than Kate's entire wardrobe.

"You can wear mine," Kate said.

Angela struck a pose and spanned her tiny waist with both hands. "It'll be way too big."

"Not when you tie the number around it."

As if on cue, the sales clerk approached with three

navy hunt jackets draped over her arm. One of them had a red velvet collar. Eagerly, Angela reached for it.

"No," Kate said, glancing at her watch. "You need to school Ragtime."

"Holly's doing it," Angela said.

Kate wanted to smack her. "Holly is *not* your groom."

"But *you* are my personal shopper."

Despite herself, Kate began to giggle. So did Angela. For a few giddy moments, they weren't rivals. They were two girls on a shopping spree with their mother's credit card.

"Angela," said a familiar voice behind them. "What *do* you think you're doing?"

* * *

Down came the mask on Angela's face. She turned away from Kate and seemed to shrivel into herself like a sunflower that withered the moment winter arrived.

Kate left them at the counter where Mrs. Dean slapped down several credit cards and told Angela to buy another jacket. Whatever she wanted. Boots, too. New spurs? Would that help? The smell of money overpowered Angela's perfume.

Feeling slightly sick, Kate made her way back to the

warm-up arena. Holly had Ragtime cantering over practice fences as if they were no bigger than the toy jumps in her bedroom.

"How's he going?" Kate said.

Holly pulled to a halt. "Fabulous."

Within minutes, Angela appeared. The gold buttons on her new riding jacket shone like tiny spotlights. She avoided Kate's eyes and took hold of Ragtime's reins. Holly jumped off.

"He's frisky," she said. "So watch out."

Kate gave Angela a leg-up. "Good luck."

* * *

Ragtime soared over the course like the pro he was, and Angela left the Larchwood arena with a clear round to thunderous applause. Mrs. Dean could hardly contain her excitement. She swept her red cape over one shoulder and embraced the judge. His mottled face turned the same shade as Mrs. Dean's outfit.

"Lunch," Holly said. "I'm starving."

"Me, too," Jennifer said.

They joined Adam and Brad in the cafeteria.

Both boys were tucking into huge servings of hamburgers, sweet potato fries, and onion rings. Brad wiped ketchup off his mouth.

"Did Angela win?" he said.

Kate sighed and explained the rules about qualifying for the Festival, while Holly grabbed hot dogs, soft drinks, and two garden salads. Brad was trying hard to understand, but he still didn't get it.

So Kate tried an analogy—dressage was like shredding the half-pipe where form counted for everything, and cross-country was the equivalent of downhill racing.

"Okay, I get that," Brad said, finishing off his fries. "But what about show jumping?"

Adam grinned. "That's the slalom."

"Exactly," Jennifer said, checking her watch. "But we'd better hustle. It's almost two."

* * *

Anxiously Holly crossed her fingers as Kate and Magician entered Larchwood's dressage arena. When Holly had ridden Tapestry at the last show, Kate said it was weird and wonderful all at once, watching your horse perform with someone else in the saddle. But Holly was used to it. For two years she'd sat in a wheelchair and watched others ride Magician. He'd never let her down.

And he didn't this time.

Nose tucked, ears on full alert, and legs doing what they were supposed to be doing, Magician responded to Kate's subtle commands like clockwork. He cantered perfect circles, extended across the diagonal, and walked on a loose rein. This was all part of the test, but the show rules called for something extra—whatever the rider wanted—so Kate and Magician threw in a couple of flying changes that had the audience on its feet.

Holly's cell phone buzzed.

Mom!

Aunt Bea came to the rescue.

"Let me talk to her," she said and promptly told Liz they were at the show and that Kate had just done a brilliant job with her dressage test. She held up the phone so Liz could hear the audience cheering Kate's ride.

There was a significant pause, and Holly could picture her mother's reactions—anger, worry, and pride. With luck, there'd be enough pride to cancel out the other two and Mom wouldn't insist on driving home.

"Yes, Kate's knee is fine," Aunt Bea went on.

Another pause.

"Kate's doctor wasn't available, but her therapist gave us the go ahead," said Aunt Bea sounding firm. "Have fun, and we'll see you tomorrow." She hung up and gave Holly her phone. "Turn it off so she can't call you again."

"She'll just call you instead."

"Then she'll get my voice mail," Aunt Bea said. "I left my phone on your kitchen table. I'm afraid she'll end up talking to the fridge."

"Or the oven," Holly said, giggling.

Aunt Bea gave her a high five. "Let's hear it for silly old women who forget things."

15

DETERMINED NOT TO LIMP, Kate led Magician back to the barn. Aunt Bea had knitted him a multicolored ribbon that she insisted on pinning on his bridle even though Kate kept telling her they hadn't won anything.

"But you've qualified," Aunt Bea said.

"Not yet," Kate replied, rubbing her knee. It had started acting up when she was halfway through her dressage test. Holding it all together for that last flying change had been a challenge.

Holly chimed in. "We won't know the final results until Monday afternoon."

While Kate untacked Holly's horse and showered him with kisses and carrots, Mr. Evans assured Brad that he didn't need to return the trailer right away. "Pardner and me ain't going nowhere," he said, patting Aunt Bea's arm. "Would you like to drive back with me?"

"Definitely," she said. "My hips won't take another ride in Brad's truck."

"Coward," Holly said, grinning.

Aunt Bea threatened to smack her with a skein of yarn, then followed Kate and Holly to the barn's entrance where they waited for Mr. Evans and his car—an enormous black Cadillac with sheepskin seat covers, steer horns on the front bumper, and a sound system that blared country music.

Dolly Parton rocked the airwaves as Mr. Evans opened the passenger door for Aunt Bea. Holly said the car would probably show up in her next book. "Driven by *The Rhinestone Cowboy*," she added.

Aunt Bea waved. "I loved that song."

"Huh?" Kate said.

"Before your time," Holly said and snapped off a photo. In less than a minute she had it up on the barn's Facebook page along with the videos she'd taken of Kate and Magician.

"Did you take one of Angela?" Kate said.

Holly shook her head. "No, but I bet Mrs. Dean did."

* * *

An hour later, they watched Ragtime carry Angela through a flawless dressage routine. Kate had mixed emotions. She liked this crazy horse and wanted him to qualify.

Earlier, when nobody was looking, she'd fed Ragtime a peppermint Life Saver in his stall. He snarfed it up and wanted the whole pack. But she'd held off. It wasn't right to feed candy to someone else's horse.

But she'd done it with Buccaneer.

Last summer he'd exploded out of the horse trailer at Timber Ridge like a wild thing and nobody could get near him—not even Liz—until Kate discovered his passion for Life Savers. After that, he was putty in her hands.

Where was he now?

His flamboyant owner, Giles Ballantine, the movie director, had shipped Buccaneer to his farm out west as soon as they finished filming at Timber Ridge. The last Kate heard, he'd been sold overseas.

The barn began to empty out as horses and riders headed for their trailers and the long journey home. A Larchwood groom led Ragtime into his stall, removed his tack, and rubbed him down. A few minutes later, Angela showed up alone. No sign of Mrs. Dean. She was probably in Larchwood's hospitality suite, drinking cocktails and boasting about Angela's performance.

Angela cleared her throat. She looked at everything except Kate and said, "You qualified."

The edges of Kate's world blurred. Nothing seemed to move. No horses clattered down the aisle, no shouts echoed from the tack room. Not even a renegade swallow swooped from the barn's pristine rafters.

"How do you know?" Holly said.

"The judges told my mother."

"What about you?" Holly said. "Did you qualify?"

"Yes."

Kate finally caught her breath. "Why are you telling me this?"

"Because I don't like owing favors," Angela said. "And now we're even." Without another word, she turned and walked off.

Don't miss **Book 8** in the exciting
Timber Ridge Riders series,
coming in January, 2014

Double Feature

With Valentine's Day, the *Moonlight* premiere in
New York, and an important horse show
coming up, Kate McGregor and her best friend
Holly Chapman have a lot to look forward to.

Or dread.

Kate's convinced neither of the guys she likes
will send her a card, Holly's obsessing over what
to wear for the movie premiere, and both girls
are anxious about the horse show.

With good reason.

Angela Dean and her new horse, Ragtime, are
bound to steal the limelight and Angela will stop
at nothing to get it. To make matters worse, she's
insanely jealous because Kate and Holly have
been invited to the big *Moonlight* premiere and
she hasn't.

Will Angela find a way to steal the limelight
there as well?

Sign up for our mailing list and be among the first to know when the next Timber Ridge Riders book will be out.

Send your email address to:
timberridgeriders@gmail.com

For more information about the series, visit:
www.timberridgeriders.com

Note: all email addresses are kept strictly confidential

About the Author

MAGGIE DANA'S FIRST RIDING LESSON, at the age of five, was less than wonderful. She hated it so much, she didn't try again for another three years. But all it took was the right horse and the right instructor and she was hooked.

After that, Maggie begged for her own pony and was lucky enough to get one. Smoky was a black New Forest pony who loved to eat vanilla pudding and drink tea, and he became her constant companion. Maggie even rode him to school one day and tethered him to the bicycle rack . . . but not for long because all the other kids wanted pony rides, much to their teachers' dismay.

Maggie and Smoky competed in Pony Club trials and won several ribbons. But mostly, they had fun—trail riding and hanging out with other horse-crazy girls. At horse camp, Maggie and her teammates spent one night sleeping in the barn, except they didn't get much sleep because the horses snored. The next morning, everyone was tired and cranky, especially when told to jump without stirrups.

Born and raised in England, Maggie now makes her home on the Connecticut shoreline. When not mucking stalls or grooming shaggy ponies, Maggie enjoys spending time with her family and writing the next book in her TIMBER RIDGE RIDERS series.